FOLLOWERS

ANNA DAVIES

POINT HORROR

ISBN 978-0-545-51196-4

Library of Congress Cataloging-in-Publication Data Available

12 11 10 9 8 7 6 5 4 3 14 15 16 17 18 19/0

Printed in the U.S.A. 40

First edition, January 2014
Book design by Natalie C. Sousa

Dedicated to Mrs. Russo's CHS Shakespeare class. This book is proof that I absolutely should have been the allusion contest winner in 2000. Ah-yoos forever!

CHAPTER 1

Briana Beland @alleyesonbree
At machale and ready for some drama.
#hamletauditionstomorrow!

I clicked TWEET and stared down at my avatar, looking up at me from my tiny iPhone screen. The picture was a headshot from last summer, sent in with my MacHale application even though the admissions form made it clear that a photo — let alone a professional shot complete with hair and makeup — was unnecessary. The girl in the photo had sparkly brownish eyes with a rim of gold around the edges, a wide smile, and blondish hair perfectly blown straight over her shoulders. She looked confident, assured, the type of girl who felt school-play auditions were worthy of an exclamation mark.

I hated her.

A flurry of good-luck Tweets flew in from Annie, Carolyn, Brittany, and Katy — all of my friends from Wright Memorial High School, but they did little to soften the knot of anxiety calcifying in my stomach. I appreciated their support, but their well-wishes couldn't sit next to me in the MacHale dining hall. Their "positive vibes" wouldn't choose me as a tennis partner instead of forcing me to spend forty-five minutes making awkward conversation with Coach Ruth as I missed serve after serve. Right now, all that mattered were my new classmates.

The only problem was that I didn't seem to matter to them. I swiped my phone to refresh the feed. Nothing.

"Are you studying your monologue back there, honey? We still could run some lines if you feel that would be helpful. You know I love to see you perform. Can you just do a little bit of it? For me?" My mom craned her neck back toward me, the jangling of her gold earrings breaking up the otherwise silent car trip.

"That's okay, I think I've got it. But thanks!" I added perkily. Or at least, that's what I was going for. It was a very good thing that I wasn't auditioning for a teen romantic comedy. I don't fake perky well.

Mom shot me a hurt gaze. I felt a familiar twinge of guilt at having disappointed her. It wasn't my fault I wasn't the animated, always-the-center-of-attention drama queen she'd been in high school. But she seemed to act like it was.

I glanced out the window to avoid eye contact. In the past hour, the sky had gone from shadowy twilight to inky black, and I had no sense of what direction we were headed. I wanted to enjoy the silence, not have my mom begin her inevitable barrage of questions: *Who else was auditioning? What did Dr. Spidell say before break? Have you been practicing speaking in a lower octave? You know it creeps up when you get nervous, which can make you sound shrill.*

"Can you at least tell me what play it's from?" Mom asked eagerly. "It can't be healthy for you to keep everything bottled up like that. Come on, just tell me. I won't say anything."

"Dad? Are we almost there?" A pleading note was evident in my tone. Dad was more like me: quiet, thinking, not always *saying* every single thing that popped into his head. While I loved my mom, living with her was exhausting.

Had been exhausting.

"Fine." Mom heaved an exaggerated sigh. "I guess it's a crime to care about my only daughter's interests. I'm sorry."

"Give her a break," Dad said, as though I weren't two feet behind him. He rested his hand on Mom's knee. "And remember, we are talking about *her* interests."

Mom huffed derisively. I felt a tug of affection toward Dad, at the same time wishing for the hundredth time that I'd just taken a train up to MacHale from Connecticut. While deep down, I appreciated my mother's almost obsessive interest with my high school theater career, it didn't negate the fact her presence made me feel nervous and jumpy.

"You know, if I were auditioning for a Shakespeare play, I would choose something from *A Winter's Tale*. It's one of those ones directors don't hear very often, so they'll automatically pay more attention than if you were doing another ridiculous *Romeo and Juliet* monologue. That type of decision shows you aren't afraid to make your own choices. Back at the theater, I'll *always* let someone read to the end if it's a piece I haven't heard recently."

"I know, I thought of that," I said. In addition to her job as a pharmaceutical sales rep, Mom was also a volunteer at the local community theater, directing the two plays the theater put on each year. Invariably, they'd star Dr. Winters, my former orthodontist, who was also a talented tap dancer, and some rising high school theater star who'd then go on to major in drama at UConn. The theater itself was the multipurpose room of the local rec center, and opening-night parties for the cast were held in our basement. Not like you would know from hearing my mother talk about it. She treated her small community theater as if it were just a step below Broadway.

"Also, I'm surprised that Dr. Spidell chose *Hamlet* for Winterm. It's so long. I mean, of course it's a classic, but I don't know why you can't do something like *Guys and Dolls* or *Carousel*. Something fun. Part of me would love to go to his office and tell him that, but I know you wouldn't let me, would you?" She asked hopefully, as if she didn't know the answer to the question. Which was *No, absolutely not* and *Are you kidding me?*

Luckily, before I had to think up some sort of *Thanks but no thanks* response, I spotted the small white hand-painted sign marking the turnoff to MacHale. Or, if you read the sign: M CH. The harsh Maine winters had caused the other letters to peel away, making it virtually impossible to find the path unless you were looking for it.

"Dad, turn!" I said.

Instantly, Dad took a sharp turn that caused me to slide against the door.

"Greg, be careful!" Mom admonished, carefully patting her shoulder-length blonde hair into place.

"Oops, sorry about that," Dad said sheepishly as he slowed the car to a five-mile-an-hour crawl.

The gas lamps lighting the entrance were unlit, and the security guard wasn't standing at his usual post inside the circular guardhouse that flanked the iron-gated entrance to the school.

"Is it always this dark around here? You don't walk around alone, do you?" Dad asked nervously as he continued up the steep hill toward the castle-like complex of dorms in the center of campus. Above us, the trees creaked from the inches of snow that had accumulated on their spindly branches.

"Greg, she's fine!" Mom said. "This is MacHale. It's safe."

"I wonder if that girl's parents said the same thing," Dad muttered. "What was her name again?"

"Sarah Charonne. And I'd prefer we didn't talk about her," my mom said tightly.

Mom and Sarah had crossed paths, briefly. Mom had been a senior when Sarah, a freshman, had disappeared from campus during finals week. For a long time, everyone assumed she'd run away. After all, she'd been on the verge of failing most of her classes, and rumors had swirled that she was dating a townie her parents hated. I'd never even heard of her until this past August. That was when, five days before fall semester started, her remains had been found in the woods near the Runnymede River dam. The police had allegedly questioned a few of the people she'd associated with, including a mechanic in town who'd gone on a few dates with her, but none of the questions had led to any suspects.

But even though there weren't any real leads didn't mean people weren't suspicious. The discovery had stirred up the already uneasy relationship between the town of Forsyth and the school. MacHale kids were always snobby about the working-class town that housed the school, but the discovery of Sarah's body had made things even more icy.

"Sarah Charonne." My mother sighed. "She shouldn't have even been a student at MacHale. All that girl did was hang out with townies. She didn't make herself a part of the community. Everyone at MacHale looks out for each other. She didn't have anyone, poor girl."

Mom glanced at me in the rearview mirror as I slunk down lower in my seat. I wondered what she'd think if she knew my own socializing habits at MacHale, which, even after a semester on campus, were pretty nonexistent. But all that was about to change. It *had* to. That's why butterflies had been in perpetual motion in my stomach since the day I'd found out the winter play was going to be *Hamlet.* I needed to play Ophelia. Because, after four months of almost anonymity, I was done playing the new girl.

"Don't get me wrong, I *am* glad you're doing the winter play. Winterm used to be my favorite few weeks. You had all the fun of school without the school part. And it'll be fun even if you *don't* get a part. Besides, it'll show Dr. Spidell you're committed."

"I *know*, Mom." Fewer students came back for Winterm, giving me the ideal opportunity to make my mark. By the time the play opened on the first Friday of spring semester, I'd finally have a core group of friends and solidify my spot as a future star in the MacHale theater department.

I knew it wouldn't be an easy road. After all, most people who came to MacHale started as freshman. Anyone who transferred specifically for an extracurricular like theater had probably at least performed in one school play at their previous high school. But I couldn't have done that. Not with Mom watching.

It hadn't always been that way. When I was little, performing was one of the few ways I could get my mother's attention. I'd beg to put on shows for her friends, spend every single car ride to and from school belting out show tunes, and would try on various accents when we were out in public. Until, one time, a casting director had overheard me speaking in a Southern drawl while tagging along after my mom through the grocery store. For most people, that would be the story of how they got started.

For me, that was the beginning of the end of my so-called acting career. As soon as that casting director had pressed his card into my mom's palm, she'd sprung into action, dragging me from commercial auditions to modeling agencies to acting coaches, where my face (too generic), my personality (too nice), and my voice (too Muppet-y, whatever that meant) were pulled apart.

By middle school, I'd made it clear I was done with acting. I never appeared in any of the plays my mother directed and would always find excuses not to come to the shows. I joined the photography club and tried out for the swim team. I'd spend hours at my friends' houses. It wasn't a bad life. In fact, it was pretty good. But I knew that *something* was missing. After all, I still thought about theater all the time, devoured every play we had to read in English class, and wondered how I could ever attempt it without my mother knowing.

And then, bizarrely, last winter, I'd realized the best way to get out from my mother's shadow was to follow in her footsteps.

My mother and I had just attended a one-on-one guidance counselor meeting meant to help sophomores figure out how to maximize their high school careers. My guidance counselor had blinked at me several times

"I don't think I've ever seen you before," she'd said finally, as she shuffled papers around. "You must really blend in!"

She'd meant it as an icebreaker, but my mother heard it as a moral failing.

Later that night, I'd overheard my mom's voice wafting through the heating vents of my bedroom. "She needs to develop her character, Greg. She needs to learn how to define herself on her own terms. She's so . . . *blah*."

It was more an exhalation than an actual word, a deep and cutting sigh imprinted on my brain. *Blah.* It was the opposite of how I felt when I was alone. It was the opposite of how I felt when I read plays under the covers, mouthing the monologues under my breath. But it was who I'd become, especially under my mom's shadow. And if I wanted something to change, I needed to change it.

The next day, I'd spent my lunch period researching boarding schools with good theater programs. Of course I'd heard endless stories about my mother's life at MacHale — the school plays, the secret parties, the middle-of-the-night runs to Deli-C. But I'd usually tune them out. I mean, how could I fit in at the same type of school my mom loved?

Or at least that's what I thought before I clicked on the MacHale website.

The Maine Difference, the red headline boldly stated in sixteen-point type, over a photograph of smiling teenagers mid–snowball fight. And when I clicked on the arts tab, I knew this would be the perfect place for me. I could imagine myself in the homey, barn-style theater-in-the-round where shows were performed. I loved that the drama program had an emphasis on Shakespeare. And though I'd never admit it, I loved that the theater director, Dr. Spidell, wore an elbow-patched jacket in his faculty photo, just like I'd imagined a theater teacher would. And I loved that I would no longer be scrutinized by my mother.

Once I was accepted, Mom's skepticism turned into pure enthusiasm. She'd been the one to encourage me to apply to live in her old dorm, Rockefeller, and she'd presented me with her own MacHale trunk, full of vintage MacHale insignia–printed clothing, as a going away present. During the past semester, she'd made the eight-hour drive up to campus no less than five times. I knew she meant well. But I also knew that living under her microscope wasn't doing me any favors in figuring out who I was and where I belonged.

Because the fact was, deep down, I worried that my mother was correct. Maybe MacHale *wasn't* a good fit. Maybe it was the perfect school for someone louder, bubblier, more sure of herself.

After all, I'd been there for four months, and I still didn't know if I fit in. My new classmates seemed like they'd come from a different planet, full of inside jokes, shared histories, and odd traditions.

I wasn't a loner, exactly. I had people to study with or run to Deli-C on the edge of campus for emergency ice cream with. My dorm mates and I pulled all-nighters in the hallway to finish final papers in December. And just before break, I'd accompanied my roommate, Willow, to the piercing parlor in town and watched as she got a delicate silver hoop threaded through her nostril. But I still felt more like an extra than a star. When I played a small part in the one-act theater festival in October, I'd gone back to the dorm only to see on Twitter that everyone else was at a cast party that I hadn't heard about. In November, the only "happy birthday" I'd gotten on my Facebook wall from anyone at MacHale had been from my academic advisor.

We crested the hill and slowly drove around Daniels Pond. The ice glittered in the moonlight and I involuntarily shivered.

Mom rolled down the windows. "I love this scent!" she said enthusiastically, pushing her head out the window as though she were a golden retriever. "Hello, MacHale!" she shouted, her voice echoing in the wind.

"Mom!" I reddened, even though no one seemed to be around.

"Well, you're no fun." Mom pouted, even as she pulled her head in and rolled the windows up.

"Where's your dorm again?" Dad craned his neck to look at me.

"Rockefeller. Keep going."

"It's the one that looks like the *Cinderella* castle, Greg," Mom said, as if that differentiation would be at all helpful to my father.

"It's, like, the one that's not quite at the top of the hill," I clarified.

"That's where I lived my junior year, too." Mom's eyes glazed over in happy reminiscence. "I lived there with Lucy Gordon. She and I hung black curtains and then got violet lightbulbs. We called our room —"

"Studio 54. I know, you've told me a million times."

Mom ignored me.

"Well, we called it Studio 54 because it was *ironic*. We were playing Phish and the Grateful Dead all the time. It was really the hippie haven, but we thought we were being clever."

"Did any gentlemen pay a visit to Studio 54?" Dad teased.

"No! Of course MacHale would *never* allow unsupervised fraternizing between a male and a female. Isn't that right, Briana?" Mom asked with a showy wink.

I didn't have the heart to tell Mom I wouldn't know. She was the type of parent who would have been proud if I had spent the first semester cutting class to make out with members of the football team. Instead, I hadn't made out with anyone and spent most of my extracurricular time trying to avoid my room when I knew that Willow and her boyfriend were there.

At that moment, Dad pulled under the stone archway leading to the dorm entrance. He turned off the ignition.

"Ready, Briana?" Mom opened the car door and stamped her feet on the packed snow. She turned eagerly to the Rockefeller entrance.

"You guys can just leave me here. I'll be fine!" I said hurriedly as I undid my seat belt and climbed out of the car. I knew if I gave my mom any sort of encouragement, she'd be begging Ms. Robinette, our housemistress, for a rollaway cot so she could sleep over in our dorm room. *No thank you.*

"Well, at least let us come in and say hello to Willow and the gang if they're around!"

I suppressed a grimace. There was no *Willow and the gang*. There was Willow, her friends, and sometimes, depending on if I was in the room at the time and if they realized I was actually *there*, me.

"I don't think they are," I fibbed. In fact, I had no idea. The only text I'd gotten all break had been from Leah Banks, a puppyish freshman who'd also been a part of the fall series of one-acts. She'd wanted to know if she should prepare her audition in Shakespearean English or the easy-to-understand text printed on the opposite side of the page.

"Okay, then." Dad fumbled in his pocket and pulled out his worn leather wallet. A gust of cold air made me shiver. I still hadn't gotten used to the cold here, at least a full ten degrees lower than back home.

Finally, he pulled out a check. Squinting, he propped it against the dashboard, writing his name in loopy black script and leaving the amount blank.

"In case you need to —"

"Buy some snacks!" Mom offered chirpily. "If Al is still at Deli-C, ask for the Marisa Melt. It's delicious. They invented it for me."

Great. I didn't have any friends and my mom had a sandwich named after her.

"Use the cash I gave you earlier if you need to take a taxi or something," my dad finished. "I'm serious. I know this is a safe school and I know I'm playing the overprotective dad here, but I don't want you to make any dumb mistakes. Don't go walking alone into town."

I folded the check and shoved it in my pocket.

"I won't." As Dad hauled my heavy duffle out of the trunk, I caught a glimpse of myself in the side mirror. My hair, normally honey blonde, now lay dark and loose around my shoulders. I'd dyed it over break, hoping it would make me look more like Ophelia, but all it did was make me look exhausted

Dad caught my eye. "I'm proud of you, Briana. You know that, right?"

"I'm proud of you, too, honey. Of course I am," Mom said, as though she were trying to convince herself. "I just want you to get the part you want."

"And have fun," Dad said as he pulled me into a bear hug. Mom squeezed my shoulder as she slid back into the car.

"She'll have fun when she can really just *relax*. She's still so self-conscious," I heard Mom murmur as she slammed the door. I slung my bag over my shoulder, then fished my key card out of my pocket and waved it over the electronic lock pad. I didn't look behind me as I headed inside the dorm.

The walnut archways and banisters had clearly been polished, and vacuum tracks were evident on the green carpets. The pillows on the antique low-slung couches in the parlor had been plumped. The lobby looked — and sounded — like an exhibition at a museum. Normally, there was an undercurrent of pop music and cell-phone rings wafting through the walls, forming a teen-girl soundtrack. Today, everything was silent.

I crossed my fingers, hoping that I was the first person back. After the car ride and long journey down Mom's memory lane, I was looking forward to being by myself, pulling out my in-case-of-emergency bag of Hershey's Kisses from my desk drawer and crawling under the covers to go over my monologue a few more times.

Unfortunately, as soon as I turned the corner toward the junior corridor, I heard the sound of high-pitched laughter coming from my room. *Great.*

I pushed the door open, knowing it wouldn't be locked.

"Hey," I said tentatively, noting that while Willow was lounging solo on her bed, my bed had *three* occupants: Tristan Schuler was sitting on my pillow, while Chad Connor and Tad Richman were both slouched against the wall.

"Yo." A voice from the corner made me whirl around. Eric Riley, sitting cross-legged on the rug, smiled up at me. Heat rose to my cheeks. Eric was a senior, the star of every MacHale play, and the recipient of several statewide theater awards. He looked like a football player, wrote songs he played at the Upper Deck coffee shop in town on Friday nights, and had made me cry when he played John Proctor in last year's production of *The Crucible*. Of course he was going to play Hamlet. I'd spent the entire break imagining performing across from him. So much so, in fact, that seeing him in person made me blush, as if he'd somehow be able to tell that I'd fallen asleep almost every night scripting imaginary conversations with him about life, Shakespeare, and the enigmatic fish tattoo on the base of his thumb. He was wearing shorts, which was slightly odd given the fact that it was twenty degrees, but what was most striking was that he was all by himself. Usually, he was joined at the hip with Skye Henderson, a sophomore theater star and the other half of Riled Up, which was what Eric called his folk-rock act.

"Hey," Chad and Tad said in the same breath, not bothering to look up from the iPad balanced on the bed between them.

"Hey . . . guys." I could never tell Chad and Tad apart. The first time I'd met them I'd assumed they were twins. They had similar broad shoulders, floppy Irish setter–colored hair that fell perfectly over one eye, dimples in their strong chins, and an expansive bow tie collection that they drew from when they performed with the MacHale a capella group.

"So, you're a castaway with us? Welcome! Love the hair!" Tristan jumped up from the bed and embraced me in a tight hug. I stiffened. Tristan was editor in chief of the *MacHale Crier* and the heir to the Animal Instincts line of frozen soy nuggets. He was involved in student government, the alumni board, and the MacHale Arts Appreciation Club. He and

Willow had a love-hate relationship with each other, and Willow usually declared him bourgeois, which was the biggest insult she'd use on anyone. Clearly, though, something had changed between them. I cautiously hugged him back.

"Welcome back," Willow drawled, as though I'd just returned from French class, not two weeks of winter break. Willow was never surprised by anything, and never felt she had to explain anything — like why MacHale's hottest guys were lounging around our bedroom. I sometimes would come back to the room and find all the furniture rearranged because she felt it was better for the room's energy flow. Other times, I'd find her typing a paper wearing only a bra and underwear because she felt clothes were too constricting when writing about art. And, of course, I'd come home more than a few times to find a nearly naked guy sitting at her desk while she stood in front of a canvas, squinting and wondering aloud whether his ab muscles were too defined in her rendition.

I felt like I'd crashed a party.

"Is it cool if I stay?" I found myself asking as I shrugged off my duffle.

Willow laughed easily. "It's your room. Of course."

"Right. Sorry." I looked around for a place to sit. The middle of the floor was covered in stray papers, sketches, and a large bowl of popcorn. The only place available was next to Eric. Where was Skye? And then I felt a sudden, unexpected thrill of excitement. If she wasn't here, then . . .

"Eric looks lonely. You should sit next to him," Tristan said, as if he'd read my mind. "How's the single life going, man?"

My ears pricked up at the word *single*. Eric shifted uncomfortably.

"It's good. Skye and I are still friends, I guess. We're just taking a break."

"Have you ever heard of a break actually working?" Tristan used his fingers to make exaggerated air quotes around the word *break*. "Don't insult my intelligence. You and Skye are donzo. What do you think? Will you comfort our tragic hero?" Tristan swiveled toward me.

I blushed, unsure of what to say. Tristan spoke like a smart and funny Twitter feed, as though every single thought he had was distilled and delivered in 140 characters of snark.

"Don't scare my roommate away. Tristan's just being an idiot. Sit wherever you want," Willow said, coming to my rescue.

I shot her a grateful glance as I picked my way toward Eric. Just as I settled onto the floor, twisting my left knee under my right thigh to make sure my legs didn't accidentally brush Eric's, my phone buzzed.

I pulled it from my back pocket. My knee slammed against Eric's. I jerked back, as though I were hit with an electric shock.

> **Tristan Schuler**
>
> The real #machaledrama? Realizing I stole @alleyesonbree's bed. #sorrynotsorry

I looked up at him as a devilish grin formed on his face. I hadn't even realized he followed my Twitter. I'd started it back in the fall, mostly to make it sound like I was having a far better time at MacHale than I actually was. It had never occurred to me that actual MacHale students read it.

My phone buzzed again.

Tristan Schuler

Somehow I think @alleyesonbree is OK with the seating arrangement. ;)

"No!" I protested out loud, aware I was blushing. Tristan shrugged.

"What's going on?" Eric tried to glance over my shoulder, but I twisted away, then began to type, my fingers flying over the keys as though they were possessed.

Briana Beland @alleyesonbree

First night back and Tristan is already starting trouble. #dramadramadrama

I felt a surge of adrenaline as I pressed TWEET. Instantly, Tristan's phone chirped. I'd never had any of Willow's friends — or frenemies, for that matter — single me out before. I wasn't sure if it was because it was break, because they felt bad about taking over the room, or because there just weren't any other options, but I didn't want to ask questions.

"What are you doing to this poor girl? She's getting all hot and bothered." Eric tried to grab my phone as blood surged to my cheeks. I knew I was bright red and felt sweat prickling the back of my neck. My brain felt sticky, moving from one thought to another half a second too slow. Tweeting with Tristan had been easy. But talking in front of everyone seemed almost impossible.

"Uh," I started, feeling like my brain and mouth weren't connected.

"We're having a Twitter war. Bree started it." Tristan smiled at me.

"I knew she was trouble as soon as she sat down next to me. Don't worry, I'll keep her in line," Eric said.

"Ew. I *hate* Twitter." Willow flopped from her stomach to her back, letting her head fall over the side of the bed so she was staring at us like an upside-down bat. "It's bourgeois. It's like, who wants to hear you brag about what you ate for lunch?"

"If it's the Marisa Melt at Deli-C, then my mom cares a lot." I heard the words come out of my mouth without fully realizing I'd said them.

"Sorry, I didn't mean anything about *your* Twitter feed. I'm sure it's cool!" Willow said encouragingly.

"No . . . it's just . . . I mean . . ." I trailed off. I wanted to explain to her that I wasn't talking about myself, I was talking about my weird mom. But then I'd have to explain her MacHale obsession, her pushiness, the fact that she thought Willow and I were best friends when we were really acquaintances with similar sleep schedules. "My mom has a sandwich named after her at Deli-C and loves talking about it," I said finally. "She was babbling about it on the car ride up."

"Are you kidding?" Chad — or Tad — asked, actually looking at me for the first time. "That's so cool! I want a sandwich to be named after me. What's her secret?"

I shrugged. "Don't know. I guess just be memorable? Be friendly to the deli guys? Have weird taste?"

"I bet you can do better than that. I bet you could get a *wrap* named after you," joked Tristan.

"All right!" The guy closest to me whooped. So that must be Chad. Chad, I realized, was the one with almost brown hair and bushy eyebrows inching toward unibrow status.

"Wraps are for wimps. I want a panini named after me," Tad said.

"I'm not talking to you," Tristan said. "I'm talking about All Eyes on Bree."

Instantly, everyone's heads swiveled toward me.

"It's my Twitter handle," I said quickly. It was embarrassing to hear it spoken out loud. I'd liked the way it looked on screen, but when I heard it, it made me sound self-absorbed and spotlight-crazy.

"Follow her," Tristan said knowingly. "It's where you can also find fun facts like Briana's recent adventures into the dark side of hair color. I *love* the chocolate. I think you were right not to go red." Tristan grabbed a section of my hair and let it fall over my shoulder. "Sometimes, basic turns out to be the more adventurous option."

"You're the one who's adventurous," I said, taking note of the peacock-blue streak in his jet-black hair.

But Tristan wasn't listening. He was scrolling through his feed instead. "Oh yeah, you had that awesome one about how freshmen with care packages are worse than kindergarteners at show-and-tell."

"Right. Because they're, like, *waving* around the boxers their moms sent them as if it's this flag of independence. They're so clueless it's cute." I was glad someone else appreciated the weirdness that surrounded us on an almost daily basis at MacHale.

"Wait, what's your handle again?" Chad asked, furrowing his eyebrows — or, I guess, eyebrow — as he whipped out his phone.

"Um . . . All Eyes on Bree."

"Wait. So you're Bree and not Briana? Why didn't you tell me that?" Willow asked.

"You didn't know your roommate's *name*?" Tristan asked in mock incredulity.

Because *I* didn't know I'd always wanted to be the type of person who had a nickname, but so far, no one had seemed to care enough about me to come up with one. But who said I couldn't come up with one myself?

I smiled. "You didn't ask. But yeah, you guys can call me Bree if you want."

Call me anything, just don't call me late for dinner! One of my dad's stupid jokes floated through my head. Hopefully the cooler, shorter name would come with a brain that was less of a social liability.

"Bree. Got it."

I nodded, silently agreeing with Willow. Briana was hesitant, questioning, afraid to correct people when they dragged out the middle *a*. No one could question Bree.

Willow nodded. "Like the cheese. I dig it."

"Like the cheese," Eric repeated. I couldn't tell if he was making fun of me. A silence hung in the air, and I wondered if that was my cue to leave. I pushed myself to my feet.

"Anyway, I've got to go work on my monologue," I said.

"But we were having a nice time!" Tristan protested. "Is this your polite way of saying you want us to leave your room?"

"No, it's fine, it's just . . . auditions tomorrow. You know."

Chad and Tad nodded solemnly. Not like they had to worry. More girls than guys *always* auditioned, and *Hamlet* was full of guy parts. They'd be fine.

"Why'd you have to bring that up? I was trying to forget about it, Bree," Eric groaned.

"Sorry!"

"No, I needed someone to give me a reality check. I should really go rehearse." Eric rose to his feet. It was weird to see him in my bedroom, the way he was standing next to my haphazard pile of shoes, how the photos I'd placed at eye level were at his chest. *Larger than life.* Or at least, larger than *my* life.

"Do you want to do it together?" I regretted the words as soon as they left my mouth. "You don't have to!" I added hastily.

He nodded slowly. "That'd be great. Thanks."

The way he said it made it sound like I was the one doing him a favor. I blushed.

"Just don't let him read the Juliet parts. He'll want to. Trust me," Chad joked, causing Tad to snort.

"It's *Hamlet*, idiot," Eric said good-naturedly. "And I only play Juliet when I'm with you."

"Well, you guys should go now." Tristan peered out the window. "Robinette's office light is still on."

"All right. Let's make our getaway." Eric picked up his coat from the floor and pulled it over his shoulders.

"We're going outside?" I asked in surprise. I'd assumed we'd just head down to the parlor, the one spot in the dorms where co-ed fraternizing was allowed to occur.

"Yeah. Let's go to the theater. That's where we're going to audition, right? Might as well start at the scene of the crime.

My stomach flipped. Sneaking out was no big deal. I knew Willow did it all the time. And while she never mentioned where she was going, she never tried to conceal what she was doing. But I'd never actually left the dorms without signing out, and I'd certainly never snuck out with a cute guy.

"Bree?" Eric's voice pulled me out of my reverie.

"Sorry!" I chirped.

"I thought I'd lost you there for a second. You ready?"

"Yes." I grabbed my jacket from where I'd shrugged it off on the floor and glanced down at my outfit. My shirt was wrinkled and my jeans still bore the remnants of two snack stops, but I didn't have much of a choice. And besides, whereas Briana would spend hours obsessing over what to wear, Bree was effortlessly sexy. Or at least, as sexy as a girl could be with Oreo crumbs on her knees. But I couldn't stop my heart from thumping as I slid into my coat. After spending so long imagining being alone with Eric, it was finally happening. No one else seemed aware of the momentous occasion, however. In the corner, Willow squinted into the mirror as she traced liner around her eyes. Chad leaned against the wall, his eyes fixated on a random spot across the room. Tad flipped through one of our magazines. Everything was the same as it had been an hour ago, when I'd first stepped inside.

But I felt like my entire life had changed.

Tristan turned toward us, a knowing smile on his face.

"Break a leg, kids!" he said, as though he were a doofy dad telling us to have fun at our prom or something.

"Let's go." My voice was less shaky as, together, the two of us walked out of the dorm room, through the exit, and into the crisp, clear night.

CHAPTER 2

Eric Riley

Me and @alleyesonbree making Shakespeare history #worstlyricintheworld #auditions #rehearsing

"Do you really need to rehearse? You know you're the only one Spidell wants for the part, right?" I asked as the two of us made our way around the pond and toward the theater. Eric had starred in all three of the one-acts we'd done over the fall. He'd played the lead in the fall drama and the spring musical last year. "You're, like, the star of the department." My teeth chattered and I wished I were wearing my puffy blue parka instead of my bomber jacket. A Tweet flew into my head.

Fact: Acting cool deprives you of body heat.

My lips twitched upward into a smile.

"What's so funny?" Eric asked.

"Nothing, I'm just cold. Sorry." I stamped my feet on the ground for emphasis.

"Gotcha. I don't get cold." He gestured to his bare lags. "I have, like, insane body heat."

He had no idea.

"You're lucky," I said. "In lots of ways." I'd meant it as a compliment, but my inexperience at flirting was made apparent when Eric flinched.

"I don't know about that." There was a slight edge to his voice, one that warned me not to ask what he'd meant. We'd stepped onto the cobblestone path that led through the academic buildings, Scholar's Walk. The legend went that only seniors could walk from the beginning to the end. Underclassmen were supposed to step off at some point, or risk bad luck.

"So what's your deal, anyway, Bree?"

"My deal?" I asked blankly, watching my feet edge closer and closer to the end of the path.

"Yeah, your jam, your drive . . . like, who are you?"

"That's a pretty big question," I said, unsure whether he was making fun of me or not. I racked my brain for something interesting, something that would make him realize it wasn't a mistake for him to rehearse with me. "Do you have a more specific one?"

"Fair enough. Well, you're new, right? What do you think of MacHale?"

"It's a little Mac-zausting, to be honest."

Eric chuckled and I unleashed a flurry of nervous giggles.

"I hear you on that. Same people, same food, same drama, same stuff. Don't get me wrong, it's fun, but it's just a little *static*."

"Right." I was surprised he got it. I'd always thought that he and the rest of his friends were having the time of their lives at MacHale, while I was the one drifting from class to the dorm and back again. I glanced down, noting that only two slate bricks stood between us and the end of the path. I automatically stepped off. Eric didn't.

He raised an eyebrow as my foot hit the grass.

"What?" I asked defensively.

"You're superstitious, aren't you?" His tone was teasing, and I felt myself blush. Again.

"Maybe. Ish? Maybe-ish?"

"Maybe-ish. I like that. You're an interesting girl, Bree."

I was glad his back was toward me as he walked off toward the clump of trees by the theater entrance. He stopped at a bird feeder, felt around the bottom, and held up a silver key in triumph.

"Impressive." As soon as the word left my mouth, I cringed. I'd meant it seriously, but it sounded jaded and sarcastic. No wonder I'd never had much luck as an actress.

Wordlessly, he put the key into the lock and pushed open the heavy wooden door. I automatically felt along the wall for the light switch. A sliver of wood dug into my palm and I gasped. "Are you okay?"

"Splinter. I'm fine!"

I felt Eric's warm hand brush against mine just as the space was bathed in a ghostly glow of light. "Splinters are good luck. You should know that."

"According to who?" I winced as I yanked the sliver of wood from my skin, which was still warm from Eric's touch. He was right. He *did* have insane body heat.

"According to me." Eric smiled.

The two of us walked from the lobby into the auditorium. The stage was bathed in moonlight, making artificial lights unnecessary. I glanced around. I'd been in the auditorium hundreds of times before, but always when the bleachers were littered with backpacks and piles of books, when the room had a brief hum of conversation, even if a scene was going on onstage. Now the only signs of life in the space were the visible puffs of air coming from our mouths and the echoey sound of Eric's footsteps as he paced around the stage. He moved slowly, deliberately, as though he were performing some private ritual. I slipped off my jacket and watched him.

The silence wasn't awkward anymore. It felt right, like both of us were in a holy place. The auditorium was constructed like a theater-in-the-round, with ten rows of wooden bleachers surrounding all four sides of the stage. A retractable skylight above the stage allowed it to be used for afternoon performances when the weather was nice, but today, the pane of glass was covered with a light dusting of snow, causing the natural moonlight to dapple unevenly on the dark wooden stage. In the dim light, dust motes swirled through the air like snowflakes. And even though the temperature outside was freezing, someone had obviously kept the heat on in the theater — the air felt warm and dry against my skin.

Adrenaline surged through my veins. I'd been rehearsing one of Ophelia's earlier monologues, before she goes crazy, when she realizes Hamlet isn't acting like himself and she doesn't know what to do about it. She confesses to her brother, Laertes, about how weird Hamlet seems. Most people do Ophelia's later monologue, where *she's* the one everyone thinks is crazy, but I didn't like that one. I like it when she's still herself, before the madness has gotten to her. When she still thinks everything can be okay.

Whenever I performed the monologue — alone, in my room, when no one else was home — I felt I *was* Ophelia, hoping that *someone* would listen to me. I loved that moment, when I stopped thinking like Briana and started thinking like someone entirely different.

"I never really liked *Hamlet*," Eric said, interrupting my thoughts. He stood onstage still, his gaze fixed beyond me and toward the last row of the auditorium. "I mean, I know it's a classic. I know it's major. And I appreciate its role in the Shakespearean canon, but honestly, I don't get him."

"You don't get Hamlet?"

"Yeah. I mean, he has all these *plans*, but at the end of the day, he thinks he's powerless. He spends so much time thinking and hardly any time actually doing anything. It's like he's decided he's doomed from the very beginning."

"Isn't that what makes it such a strong part?" I countered as I gingerly stepped onto the stage and stood next to him. I closed my eyes, imagining the seats filled with people and the sound of applause ricocheting off the wooden walls. I crossed my fingers and made a wish. *Please.*

"I know. I mean, I want to play him. I just don't *get* him. Now, Macbeth . . . he's a guy I get."

"Eric!" I reached out and hit him hard on the arm before I even knew what I'd done. It was one of the cardinal rules of acting that you *never* said *Macbeth* inside the theater. According to theatrical legend, the play was cursed, and saying it caused bad luck. Rumors abounded about mysterious fires, injured actors, and even accidental sword deaths . . . not to mention disappointing auditions.

Eric chuckled. "Sorry. I forgot you're superstitious."

"I'm *not* . . . but it's just . . . Okay, I am. A little," I admitted.

Eric grinned. "Sorry. What am I supposed to do to fix it?"

"Turn around three times and spit over your shoulder. Outside."

Eric flicked his gaze toward the door. "Really?"

I paused. It was a silly theater superstition. I didn't *really* believe it. But it gave me a small thrill to see him indulging me, and I wanted to prolong our banter as long as possible.

Eric let out an exaggerated sigh. "I am banish*ed*," he said, purposefully misquoting

I smiled. "Get thee to the outside nunnery."

As Eric turned to leave, I walked to the center of the stage and glanced toward the lighting booth. I imagined that I was wearing a floor-skimming dress instead of jeans and a fleece. I imagined a sea of faces glancing up at me, bathed in a single spotlight. I pulled my hair out of my ponytail and shook it loose over my shoulders.

"I'm going to play Ophelia." My skin prickled as I said the words out loud. Silence surrounded me. Too much silence.

"Eric?" I called. He'd only gone out the front door; it shouldn't take him this long. I felt my heart pick up its pace. I thought of my dad's warnings: *Don't make any dumb mistakes.* Did being alone, in the theater, late at night qualify?

"Eric?" I called again, uncertainly, thinking of the *Macbeth* curse. My mom believed it; she even had signs put up backstage before her shows reminding people not to say the name of "the Scottish play" out loud. But that was my overdramatic mother, who'd do anything for a scene. She was overreacting. And now I was overreacting.

"Eric, you don't have to take forever. You can come back. It's okay." My heart pounded harder. "Eric?" My voice raised upward with the beginnings of panic.

Calm down, I told myself. Most likely, he'd been locked out. Worst-case scenario, one of the teachers roaming campus had caught him and sent him back to his dorm. I jumped off the stage and headed up the aisle. Every footfall echoed. I pushed open the heavy wooden door that led to the lobby. The lights had been turned off. The only illumination was from a shaft emanating from the gas lamp at the doorway.

"Eric?" I called, trying to sound far more confident than I felt. Nothing.

The door was still ajar. So he hadn't been locked out. I slowly peeked around the corner of the door. The snow had started coming down harder, and the trail of footprints we'd left had already been erased. Except that if Eric had gone outstide, there should have been a new set leading away from the theater. It was like I'd imagined the whole thing: asking him to rehearse, sneaking out of the dorm, walking around the bare stage.

"Eric?" The wind whipped around my ears. I squinted toward the tree line in the woods circling the campus. And there, in the distance, I saw two small, beady points of light staring back at me.

"Eric!" I shouted. I darted back to the auditorium. I tripped over the doorstop separating the lobby from the auditorium. The door slammed behind me, plunging the room into blackness.

Where are the lights? I ran my hands desperately along the walls, not caring about splinters, until my fingers closed on the switch. I desperately toggled it up and down. Nothing.

"Help!" I called desperately. "Help!"

I heard the sound of a door creaking from the direction of the theater.

"Help!" I shrieked again.

My knees buckled beneath me. Sweat or tears slicked my face.

I squeezed my eyes shut. When I opened them, the room was dimly lit. Eric stood in front of me, crystalline snowflakes laced in his dark hair like diamonds. I blinked again.

Eric gazed down at me in concern. "Are you okay? I'm sorry. I think when I went outside I must have tripped over an electrical cord or something. I went down to find the fuse box . . . and then I found you."

Was I okay? My breath was still caught in my throat, my heart still hammered in my stomach. And I'd seen *something* in the woods.

Eric leaned down to help me stand up. I flinched away from him.

"Sorry. I just feel a little skittish." I thought back to the two eyes. At the time, they'd seemed so real. But now, with the lights and the warmth and the scent of Eric's cologne-and-deodorant combination surrounding me, they seemed overdramatic and dreamlike, a sign my brain had gotten carried away. I decided not to tell him. Being scared and superstitious when the lights went off was understandable. But babbling about seeing something in the woods seemed certifiably crazy.

"I couldn't tell." Eric smiled.

"But I'm fine now. Really. Ready to rehearse?" I scrambled to my feet and discreetly wiped the tears from my face as I practically raced into the auditorium. Eric walked behind me.

"We can go rehearse in the dorm if you like. You seem really freaked out."

"No, I'm good," I lied. I headed down the steps of the stage and plopped into one of the chairs in the first row of bleachers.

"It's kind of funny, right?" My voice sounded high and reedy and not at all like my own.

Eric nodded, but didn't make any move to go onstage. "I don't know, Bree. You look like you've seen a ghost."

A ghost. I suppressed a shudder. "I'm *fine.* Seriously. We should do the monologues before it gets too late."

"Right." Still, he didn't make a move to go onstage.

"Do you want me to go first?" I asked, surprising myself.

He nodded. "I'm a little nervous about auditions. Like, I feel on the inside the way you looked when I found you in the dark. Except your panic went away when the lights went on. I'm still in my own private freak-out zone over here."

"Really?" I asked skeptically. As if someone like him would get nervous about an audition for a part he had so on lock that he could complain about how he didn't even like the character. A tiny wave of resentment rose up within me, something I never thought I'd feel about Eric — especially an Eric who'd gone out of his way to be nice to me.

"Don't worry about it," I said crisply. I strode onstage, realizing with each step that I was no longer nervous. I wanted to show Eric who I was, that I was more than some shy girl who seemed afraid of her own shadow. "Anyway, I haven't performed this in front of anyone, so don't tell me if it's terrible. Just tell me about stuff I can fix in less than twelve hours. Okay?"

Instead of waiting for an answer, I launched into the monologue, transporting myself from the barnlike theater into a misty, murky castle where nothing was what it seemed, where the only person I could trust was my brother. I imagined the clank of swords and the angry, ravaged look in Hamlet's eyes. I felt my lower lip tremble and tears spring to my eyes as I said the final line: "And to the last bended their light on me."

My heart galloped and I closed my eyes, waiting for the click when my mind would pull away from the castle and into present day. Right now, I was in what I privately imagined as the *in between*, where the character and myself were so muddled it was impossible to tell where one ended and the other began.

Eric's clapping yanked me back to present day.

I staggered toward the side of the stage, my legs shaking as I half collapsed onto one of the bleachers.

"Bree, that was amazing. Like . . . really, really good. I'd never known you were serious about this."

"I am." I let the words settle over me, and I realized that he was right. It *was* good. I knew it, certain in a way I'd almost never been before.

"So, okay, *now* I'm really nervous," Eric confessed. "I had no idea you were so talented. I've never seen you act before."

I grinned giddily as I stepped off the stage, not trusting myself to speak. I felt like I had the first time I'd gone skiing as a kid. At the end of the run, my legs still felt like jelly from nerves, but my entire body had been bursting with pride.

Eric climbed up the stage steps. "All right, well, don't judge too harshly. Same thing. If I can fix it, tell me. If not, I don't want to know," Eric said. He crossed his arms and paced. He muttered something, and I leaned forward to hear. I hadn't realized he'd already started. He smiled apologetically at me. "I'm sorry, I'm just a little nervous."

"Well, it's just me," I said, ignoring the fact that I had no proof he'd even known my name before tonight.

He nodded, as if that justification was enough to convince him. I sighed and leaned back. The transformation was complete. I was back to being *just me*. But at least he'd seen something . . . and all I had to do was bring that to the audition tomorrow for him to see it a lot more.

CHAPTER 3

Briana Beland @alleyesonbree
Mac-zausted, Mac-cited, and Mac-king a Deli-C run for carbs. #machale #hamletauditions

I pressed TWEET, then glanced at my reflection in the mirror, pleased with what I saw. I'd been playing What Would Ophelia Wear? for the past hour and had finally come up with the perfect combination of Willow's body-skimming black lace short-sleeve thrift-store dress paired with boots and black tights. I felt a little bit guilty going into Willow's closet, but she'd clearly also snuck out the night before and wasn't back in our dorm that morning. Besides, wasn't the outfit technically a costume? It was what Ophelia would wear if she shopped in a vintage store. Which Ophelia *would* do. I knew that everyone else would wear a polar fleece/sweater/jeans combo, aka the not-in-dress-code uniform of MacHale, and I wanted to stand out.

I power walked to Deli-C, running through my lines in my head. Not like I needed to. I knew them by heart. At the bagel counter, I spontaneously bought another cinnamon raisin for Eric. It was, after all, what costars did for one another.

The old man behind the counter smiled as he rang up my order.

"You're looking happy," he noted.

"It's going to be a good day." I said, plunking my change into the tip jar.

"Ah, the confidence of youth. Enjoy it while you can."

I smiled and headed out the door, bypassing the route that cut through campus and walking the long way around the perimeter. The wrought iron gates glinted in the sun. The turrets of the dorm looked like they could belong to a castle. And the faint sound of the Runnymede River as it ran behind campus could definitely be the sound of the brook Ophelia eventually drowned in.

"Briana!" A cheery voice yanked me back to reality.

I turned and blinked in surprise. Behind me was Skye Henderson, her blonde hair pulled into a shiny ponytail and her eyes perfectly lined with shimmery bronze shadow. She leaned in, clearly to go for a European-style cheek kiss, but I turned too late and caused her lip gloss to brush against my hair.

"Oops! Sorry about that!" She shrugged in a *What can you do?* gesture.

"No prob." I smiled tightly. I never knew how I should act around Skye. She and I had been put together as scene partners in Theater Arts last semester. Initially, I'd hoped her passion for theater meant we could be friends, before I realized that every single scene we did was an opportunity for her to prove that she was the best in the class. And honestly, she was good. She had wide eyes; a low, husky voice that was always on pitch; and always knew everything about the history of the plays we read. She memorized monologues for fun; had a dorm wall filled with autographed pictures and letters from Broadway actors and actresses; and even though she, like me, didn't seem to hang out with anyone on campus, she seemed too busy to care. On one hand, I admired her attitude. But not today. Especially when I'd spent the last night rehearsing with her ex-boyfriend.

"Are you nervous?" she pried. Even when she was just having a conversation, she sounded like she was acting, trying to impress a casting director who was just out of sight in another room. It was her one flaw, and one I hoped Dr. Spidell would see. One of the reasons I loved Shakespeare and felt I had a sliver of a chance was that Shakespeare *knew* how to write weirdos, outcasts, and people who talk to themselves. Sure, he was an amazing writer, but I always felt *that* was the real reason why the plays were so popular — because he actually understood how people, even kings and queens, could be awkward or sad or confused or any combination of emotions.

"Nah. I mean, I don't *think* so. Are you?"

"No. *Please.* I don't get nervous. I get *excited.* It's much better to replace a negative emotion with a positive one. But I *am* sad that —"

"You and Eric broke up?" I clapped my hand over my mouth as soon as the words left my lips, mortified to have said it out loud.

Skye blinked in surprise and shook her head. "Ugh. I *knew* that *everyone* would be talking about me and Eric. I mean, I don't *blame* them. I *know* everyone likes to gossip. But here's the thing. Even though Eric and I have decided to go our separate ways, we're still friends and still each other's number one fans." She plastered on a smile as though she'd just finished giving an interview to a member of the press. "And that's *not* why I'm upset. I'm sad about Dr. S."

"What do you mean?" I asked, forgetting momentarily about Skye and Eric.

"You didn't hear?" Skye asked in that tone of voice that meant she knew something gossipy and I didn't. "He died."

"What?" My blood turned to ice. Dr. Spidell was blustery and dramatic and always seemed like he was on the verge of a heart attack. But I couldn't imagine him *dying*. "What happened?"

Skye shrugged. "I'm not sure. Don't say anything. I guess they'll make an announcement or something. My mom heard because she's a trustee. But I guess the show must be the thing, or whatever they say."

I ignored Skye's garbled version of the phrase, trying to process the information. How could Dr. Spidell be *dead*? I'd seen him in Theater Arts only two weeks before, where he surprised us and said that instead of a final, we were going to have a party. He'd brought the entire class to his house on the edge of campus, where he'd served paprika biscuits spread with fig-and-chocolate jam. Instead of grades, he'd given everyone a copy of the Shakespeare play he personally felt they needed to read. Mine had been *Pericles*. Tears pricked my eyes as I visualized it, untouched, on my bookshelf.

"Look at you, crying on cue," Skye said approvingly. "That'll look *so* good in auditions. I try all the time, but just I can't do it!" She sighed dramatically.

We'd reached the theater doors now, and I couldn't believe I'd spent last night there, imagining what Dr. Spidell would think of the audition, when he wouldn't think anything. When he was dead.

"Dr. Spidell *died*." My voice echoed in the lobby. Groups of kids surrounded us, but the tears had blurred my vision, making it hard to see who I knew. None of them turned when I said it. Did no one care? Or did everyone know? They must not have, or else Eric would have said something the night before. It didn't matter who knew. What mattered was that he was no longer here.

"And I feel like he'd want that," Skye said solemnly.

"He'd want us to fake cry for him?"

Skye shook her head. "Not for *him*. For us. To improve our acting."

"Do you know what happened? Was it a heart attack or . . . ?"

"I mean, he was old." Skye shrugged.

Just then, a three-tone buzzer, usually meant to inform audience members that intermission had ended, dinged.

"So who's going to direct?" I hadn't even thought of the question until now.

"Hopefully someone *real*. I mean, Dr. S was nice and all, but having some high school teacher directing us isn't exactly preparing us for professional careers or anything, you know?"

Skye continued to talk, but my attention was drawn to an easel set up in the corner of the lobby. A bouquet of roses lay at its base. My skin prickled. That *definitely* hadn't been there the night before. I stepped toward it and squinted at the center photograph, of a blonde girl wearing pearls and a black sweater. It was the typical uniform for undergrad picture day at MacHale, but the photo looked faded and out-dated. I took another step.

THE MACHALE CIRCLE THEATER: DEDICATED TO SARAH CHARONNE

Underneath was another line in italicized font.

The curtain may have closed too quickly on her young life, but she will always have a place in the spotlight of our hearts.

I reached out and allowed my fingers to graze the glass frame. I traced my fingernail down to the other photos surrounding the headshot, clearly ones from past productions. I stopped at one faded and creased candid in the lower left-hand corner. According to the description, it was from a 1985 production of *Hamlet*. Sarah was in the center of the stage, her mouth open in mid-speech and her eyes radiant. She *was* in the spotlight. But my eyes drifted toward someone on the edge of the photograph. I recognized the high cheekbones, the arched eyebrow. It was my mother. Not in the starring role, but in the background. Why hadn't she told me she and Sarah had been in a play together? Why hadn't she told me she'd been in *Hamlet*?

I tore my gaze away from the photograph. It seemed like whether I liked it or not, my mother was here for my audition.

The kids around me were chattering nervously to one another, but the din was too loud for me to make out individual strands of conversation. The auditorium lobby had gotten noticeably more packed since I'd arrived, but I didn't recognize any of the people around me. Who *were* they? I knew I was the new kid, but it wasn't like MacHale was enormous.

I stood on my tiptoes and craned my neck for Eric. I spotted Vanessa Templeton, Camille Chatterjee, and Scott Eichner in one corner. They were three underclassmen I vaguely knew from acting with them as background extras in the one-act festival last year. I was about to make my way over to them when the auditorium doors opened and the kids around me poured inside. I followed them, caught up in the herd. But instead of sitting in the center section of the auditorium with them, I veered off to the left, sitting in the upper back corner of the theater. I still didn't see Eric anywhere.

Dr. Conger, the headmistress, emerged from the wings, followed by an overweight red-faced older man and a guy wearing a black sweater, skinny jeans, and sunglasses. He had blond hair that was just starting to go gray at the temples, a goatee, and looked like he belonged in some California juice bar. He certainly didn't look like a MacHale teacher.

"Hello" — Dr. Conger squinted into the lights — "and welcome back from break. As some of you may have heard, MacHale recently lost a trusted, valued, and dear friend. Dr. Spidell was loved, respected, and will be missed by our entire community. A moment of silence." Dr. Conger briefly placed her hand over her heart and looked down as the heads in front of me bowed in unison. I kept my eyes glued to the stage, sure Dr. Spidell would emerge from a trapdoor to say he was fine, that this was just a joke.

But he didn't.

"Thank you," Dr. Conger said quietly. "Next, we're thrilled to welcome Breckin O'Dell to serve as drama instructor. Mr. O'Dell comes to us by way of New York City, where he's worked extensively off and off-off Broadway. He's looking forward to upholding MacHale's tradition of excellence. And with that said, as Mr. O'Dell will soon learn, one of the hallmarks of MacHale traditions is making new ones while keeping the old."

"I thought that was the Girl Scout motto," I heard someone mutter. I snuck a glance in the direction of the voice and saw Tristan one row behind me. He raised an eyebrow and moved into the empty seat next to mine.

"What are you doing here?" I whispered.

"What does it look like?" He nodded down at his iPad. "Serious journalism. This is Pulitzer-worthy material and I'm here for the behind-the-scenes scoop. Wanna give me a quote?"

"What's in it for me?" I asked quietly before forcing my attention back to the stage.

"And with that said, I'm thrilled to announce our decision to open auditions to Forsyth High." Dr. Conger beamed as angry "What?'s" and sharp intakes of breath erupted around the room like fireworks. Forsyth was the public school, a small one-story brick building on the opposite side of town that primarily catered to the blue-collar local families who worked in the nearby restaurants, inns, and logging companies.

"My parents are paying tuition for me to hang out with *public school kids*?"

"You would think the MacHale girls would know how to dress better. I mean, have you looked at what everyone is wearing?"

"MacHale mixes with the public school. First thoughts. Go."

Snippets of conversation swirled around me as the man next to Dr. Conger was talking about the importance of an alliance between MacHale and Forsyth. He was obviously the Forsyth principal, and from the way he kept repeating the phrase *ambitious experiment*, it was clear he was just as dubious about the prospect as everyone else seemed to be.

"They all look so *smug*," Tristan whispered loudly.

"Don't you mean *snug*?" I whispered back, noticing the way the Forsyth principal's stomach strained against his shirt buttons.

"Brilliant." Tristan's fingers flew across his screen. All of a sudden, my phone buzzed.

Tristan Schuler

Turns out @alleyesonbree is as observant as her Twitter handle suggests. Spot-on observations of #forsythfashion coming your way.

"Don't!" I hissed.

Tristan shrugged. I dropped my phone and sack of bagels in my bag as butterflies crept back into my stomach and forced myself to turn my attention to the stage, where the Forsyth principal was wrapping up his speech. There were four girls I didn't know in the rows ahead of me. I crossed my fingers. *Please let them all be terrible actresses.*

"Mr. O'Dell will take it from here. We look forward to the play, and to a new, more positive chapter in the MacHale-Forsyth relationship after the sadness and confusion of this past summer's discovery," the principal said, trailing Dr. Conger offstage. A blonde Forsyth girl in front of me turned over her shoulder. Our eyes locked. I was the one who turned away first.

Mr. O'Dell strode to the edge of the stage and sat down, panning the room with his eyes. His expression didn't change, but there was something about the way his gaze landed on each of us that made me feel like we had all somehow disappointed him. Already quiet, the room became positively silent. I could hear the clock in the lighting booth tick.

Finally, he nodded. "All right. So here we are. And as your leaders have said, this is a new tradition for MacHale and —"

"Doesn't he mean MacHell?" a male voice from the back of the room piped up. Heads swiveled toward the source of the outburst. It was a Forsyth guy I hadn't seen before. He had reddish-blond hair that matched the reddish stubble on his jawline, and I couldn't help but notice the clear outline of his biceps underneath his tight flannel shirt. He looked like he was in college. And he didn't look the least bit nervous or flustered about the fact the hundred or so people now in the auditorium were all staring at him.

A half smile formed on Mr. O'Dell's face. "MacHell. I'm sure no one has ever thought of that. You must be so incredibly clever, Mr. . . . ?"

"Mathis. Zach Mathis." I winced. From his confident tone, it was obvious he was completely oblivious to Mr. O'Dell's sarcasm.

"Mr. Mathis. You may leave. Shakespeare kindly provided us fools already. Any more is a waste of time."

"Excuse me?" A red flush rapidly spreading from Zach's neck was the only clue that he was anything but confident.

"Go," Mr. O'Dell said calmly. "Can I make it any simpler?"

"I can't just go. I'm here for the audition. And I don't think you want to kick me out."

"Oooh!" one girl muttered from the audience. Collectively, everyone's head snapped toward the sound.

"Quiet!" Mr. O'Dell sputtered. "I will not have anyone take my spotlight until I give it to them. I don't care if you're Ryan Gosling. I don't care if you're John Gielgud. I don't care if you're God. You are not welcome in my theater. So good-bye and good luck."

The boy rolled his shoulders back, as though he were preparing for a fight. I swallowed, realizing that I'd been holding my breath. But then he shook his head once, grimaced, and walked out of the theater, his boots thudding ominously with every step.

Around us, there was a collective rustle; the telltale signs of iPhones subtly being pulled out, recorders turned on, photos taken. Tristan poked my arm, causing me to jump. He widened his eyes. I shook my head. Then he angled his iPad toward me.

> **Tristan Schuler**
> At least he kicked out one of the Forsyth kids. Show them the meaning of a #mac-down. (mac-down = smackdown, obviously)

I pushed his iPad away and craned my neck toward the exit. Teachers at MacHale complimented, encouraged, cajoled. They did not mock. It was terrible to watch. It was fascinating. And it was effectively taking the spotlight away from my own tangle of nerves and excitement.

"As you can see, I run a tight ship. I'm a professional, and I demand professionalism. When you're in this room, you aren't a boarding school snob or a townie or whatever you label one another. You are an artist. Is that clear?" he asked.

I squirmed. I'd just gotten an idea too irresistible not to share:

> **Briana Beland** @alleyesonbree
> "Townies make me frowny." — William Shakespeare, playwright, snob

Just then, Mr. O'Dell's gaze swiveled toward us. I paused, frozen, afraid to breathe, all of a sudden aware of how stupid I was being and furious at myself for testing my luck. For what? To get Tristan to laugh? *Dumb, dumb, dumb.*

But after a moment, Mr. O'Dell glanced away and continued to talk about the unrelenting rehearsal schedule, the complete commitment required to the play, the fact that if anyone in the theater had a second of hesitation, they should leave now. I felt Tristan nudge my leg. I shook my head and edged away from him. In the instant Mr. O'Dell's gaze had landed on us, I'd felt almost certain he was going to call us out. He'd given us a pass, and I wanted him to make sure he knew I appreciated it — that my behavior had been a split-second mistake, a moment of not paying attention.

"When you get onstage for your monologue, I don't want to see a teenager. And I don't want to see any of your own *personality*." Mr. O'Dell made a face. "I don't want to see someone worrying about Facebook or wondering whether they've gotten a text. When you get up here, I want to see the souls of kings and queens. He flung his hands wide. "This is our Wooden O. This is where we bring Shakespeare to life. It is your task to take whatever pathetic trials you're grappling with and push them aside. Shakespeare wouldn't care if you forgot to sign up for the SATs or can't find a date for Friday night. And I don't care, either. When you get up here, I want to see passion. Life. Death. Fear. Commitment. Is that clear?"

A hand shot up from the side of the theater and waved back and forth. As if anyone else was in any hurry to speak. The hand belonged to Andi Schaefer, a junior who usually ran stage crew. Her curly hair was always pulled back into a ponytail so tight it made her eyes bug out, making her look like a permanently surprised guinea pig. She was always chewing on something. Right now, the corner of her iPhone was in her mouth. A flicker of annoyance crossed Mr. O'Dell's face upon taking in her appearance.

"You don't need to raise your hand like that," Mr. O'Dell said disgustedly. "I see you. So what do you so desperately want to know? And *who* are you?"

Andi pulled her hand down, but kept her phone in her mouth, like it was a security blanket. "I'm sorry. It's just, I'm Andi Schaefer? Stage crew? And Mr. Spidell and I had *specific* conversations about me being the assistant director and I just wanted to make sure that was still happening?"

"I can't understand you with that *gadget* in your mouth. Could you please enunciate?" Mr. O'Dell asked. A single snort of uncontrolled laughter came from the middle of the auditorium.

"I said that I am usually the assistant director. I'm supposed to be. Dr. Spidell promised," Andi said, the corner of her phone still sandwiched between her lips. I was impressed that she was able to sound so confident. Did she even know Mr. O'Dell had been making fun of her?

"You're my assistant director?" Mr. O'Dell asked dubiously, as though she'd just announced that she was the newest *Vogue* cover model.

Andi nodded importantly. Mr. O'Dell offered a tight smile. Tristan snorted and began to type furiously. Seconds later, my phone buzzed.

Tristan Schuler

Here's an observation @alleyesonbree: Is this Hamlet or a new Animal Planet show starring Andi Schaefer: iPhone Eater?

I stifled a giggle as I elbowed him.

"All right. If no one else wants the position, then I guess we'll just have to make do. Would anyone else like to step up or address any other general concerns, questions, or comments?" Mr. O'Dell asked, as if he were daring anyone to actually say anything.

One hand shot up from the front of the theater. I could sense a collective intake of a breath, as if everyone couldn't believe that someone would actually take this guy up on his offer.

"Yes?" Mr. O'Dell asked with a barely controlled sneer.

"Can I go first?" It was Skye.

A slow smile spread across Mr. O'Dell's face. "A first victim. I like that. Of course. So we'll begin the auditions. Here's how it'll work. I don't care what part you want. Save that for Twitter. I will decide where you belong. Is that clear, Ms. . . . ?" Mr. O'Dell raised his eyebrow at Skye.

"Henderson. Skye Henderson. I played Helena in last year's production of *All's Well That Ends Well.* I also did a summer theater program at Sea Breeze Rep in Portland, where I played Julie in *Carousel* for two matinees."

"Two whole matinees. Impressive," Mr. O'Dell said dryly. "But as I was saying, I don't care who you are in your hormone-riddled worlds. I care about who you can become.

"Sorry. But I just wanted to let you know. Since you don't have our resumes or anything."

"Just act!" Mr. O'Dell barked.

"Okay!" Skye squeaked, heading up onstage.

My phone buzzed.

Tristan Schuler

Hey @alleyesonbree, seems like the sky might be falling . . . does that make you #riledup?

I shot Tristan a warning glance. It was one thing to make general snarky comments, but another to make it sound like I had a crush on Eric or that I was jealous of Skye. Because I didn't. And I wasn't. Or at least I didn't want anyone, even my nonexistent followers, to know that.

Sorry, Tristan mouthed.

I nodded slightly to let him know it was all right.

Everyone near us was shifting around, playing on their phones, desperately flipping through scripts. I sat with my spine ramrod straight and watched Skye's performance.

Despite Tristan's prediction, Skye was good. She performed a monologue from *All's Well That Ends Well*, clearly one she'd worked on last year. But it was honest and genuine and people laughed in certain parts of it. I bit my lip.

A few people in the audience clapped as Skye finished. Mr. O'Dell swiveled around, finally stopping his gaze on our section.

"You!"

"Me?" I croaked.

"Yes. And hurry up, please."

My legs shaking, I stood up.

"All Eyes on Bree," Tristan said approvingly. My stomach plummeted. I knew he was just trying to be supportive, but it would seem like a disruption to Mr. O'Dell.

"How nice to have a fan," Mr. O'Dell said, directing his focus squarely on Tristan. "Can you please let me know who you are and why you're in my theater? As I made clear with Mr. Mathis earlier, I'm *not* auditioning clowns. So it might behoove you to leave."

"That's cool." Tristan slung his messenger bag over his shoulder.

"Wait," Mr. O'Dell commanded.

"Yeah?"

"What's your name?"

Tristan shrugged. "I'm just an observer who can't resist a good show. And trust me, sir, this one is already amazing." With that, Tristan delivered a mock salute toward Mr. O'Dell as he turned and slunk out of the theater.

Ripples of laughter broke out around me. I turned apologetically to Mr. O'Dell, hoping he didn't think I was connected to Tristan.

"Who was that, Ms. All Eyes on Bree? Was that a friend of yours?" Mr. O'Dell's voice was smooth and deadly and caused my already weak limbs to feel even more like liquid.

"Kind of," I said, reddening. "And my name is Briana. Briana Beland. And I apologize for any disruption." The intensity of Mr. O'Dell's gaze made it clear that wasn't enough of an answer. My heart pounded harder. And then a thought crossed my mind. "He's sort of like the campus Falstaff," I said shyly. "Every Shakespeare play has a fool. And every campus has a . . . Tristan. . . ." I trailed off amid a smattering of laughter. But I didn't care about the audience. I cared about Mr. O'Dell, and right now it was impossible to gage Mr. O'Dell's reaction. "He's the editor in chief of the school newspaper. I guess he's writing about auditions or something."

"All right. Thank you for that explanation, Ms. All Eyes on

Bree Beland. You have our eyes. The spotlight is on you. What will you do with it?"

I took a deep breath, glanced up at the lighting booth, crossed my fingers for luck, and began.

"O my lord, my lord, I have been so affrighted!"

I thought back to the two eyes in the woods, imagining them watching me, feeling the fear creeping in my veins, as I imagined Ophelia felt the first time she realized that Hamlet — the person she loved most in the world — may be going mad. My voice had shaken a bit on the first two words, but the more I felt Ophelia's fear, the more the shakiness was from her own panic, not the jittery stage fright nerves I'd felt walking onstage.

The emotions crashed over me as the lines poured out. It was as if I was Ophelia, confessing to her father. It wasn't until I said the last words that I realized I'd finished.

"Thank you," I said in a small voice.

"Good," Mr. O'Dell said smoothly. I let out a sigh of relief and kept my head down as I walked back to my seat. I didn't want to see what other people thought.

I barely watched as student after student went onstage. Always, Mr. O'Dell would end their monologue with a head nod, as well as a one-syllable word: *Good. Thanks. Nice. Right.* From his tone, it was impossible to know if any of them meant anything.

Eric climbed onstage. It was the first time I'd seen him all morning. He was wearing a blue sweater over a blue-checked collared shirt and a pair of khaki shorts. Of course. His angular jaw was covered with a grazing of stubble and his eyes were bloodshot. It looked like he hadn't slept all night. Maybe he'd been more anxious than I thought. His eyes darted like a nervous deer around the auditorium. I leaned forward in my seat, hoping he'd see me. For a split second, his eyes landed on me.

It's okay, I mouthed. But then his gaze continued. I craned my neck to see who he was looking at, already knowing who it had to be.

Skye.

"To be or not to be . . ." Of course I'd heard the monologue a million times before, but Eric's rich baritone made me snap to attention. Each word was given weight, and the easy way he moved around the stage instead of standing rooted to one spot made him impossible *not* to watch.

"Thank you." Eric nodded once, then stared at the floor.

"All right." Mr. O'Dell nodded impassively, then clapped his hands twice. "I think I've had enough."

People around me sighed and started packing their bags, but Mr. O'Dell raised his finger. Everyone stopped mid-motion.

"I've seen enough *for the morning*," Mr. O'Dell clarified. "I'll read off a list of names of those who I want to see after lunch, at two p.m. sharp. Skye Henderson?"

"That's me!" Skye called jubilantly from the rear of the auditorium.

"Indeed," Mr. O'Dell said as laughter rippled around me. I grabbed one wrist with the fingers of my opposite hand, so tightly I could feel my blood whooshing through my veins at twice the speed it normally did. *Please.*

"Briana Beland?" Mr. O'Dell called. My hand fell from my wrist and I giggled in surprise. I'd made it. *I'd made it!*

Mr. O'Dell rattled off a few more names, including Eric. Not like that was a surprise. But what was surprising was how

Eric left the auditorium as soon as his name was called, his jaw set and his mouth in a firm line.

"For those of you who I've called, I'll see you at two. For those of you who I didn't . . . best of luck," Mr. O'Dell said.

"What about me?" Andi's voice called in the darkness.

"Oh. You. How about we have a brief talk? You know, to work out details. I'm thrilled to figure out what to do with you."

His tone did little to dampen Andi's enthusiasm. She practically sprinted onstage.

I grabbed my script and shoved it in my bag.

"Wanna get lunch?" a confident, cheerful voice asked, a little too loudly.

I looked up into Skye's heavily lined eyes.

"Me?" I asked.

She laughed. "Yes, you, silly! I want to talk to you!"

"Oh . . . um, okay." Part of me didn't want to go out to lunch with Skye. Part of me wanted to focus on preparing for callbacks. But another part of me felt like the audition had been more than just one for the school play. It was an audition to be accepted into the MacHale community, to be seen as someone worth getting to know. And even though I found Skye annoying and exhausting, I was flattered that she wanted to hang out with me.

The auditorium had emptied out quickly. Onstage, Mr. O'Dell was conferring with Andi, who was earnestly nodding to something she said. It felt like I was spying.

"Let's go."

"We should just go to the campus café. We only have an hour," Skye said worriedly.

I nodded, pulling out my phone so I could glance at the time.

Instead, my eye was drawn to the Tweet window at the center of my screen.

> **Hamlet's Ghost** @hamletsghost
> Seems @alleyesonbree had fun at #machalehamlet auditions. Finding humor in tragedy is a talent. . . . Can she keep it up?

I frowned.

"What?" Skye peered over my shoulder.

"Nothing." I angled my phone away from her.

"Okay." She shrugged. Together, the two of us walked toward the café. Skye was babbling about Mr. O'Dell, the auditions, and whether or not I thought he'd have us do the same monologues again, or if we'd have a chance to try something else. I nodded and made appropriate noises, but I wasn't paying attention. *Who is Hamlet's Ghost? And why is he Tweeting at me?*

We walked into the tiny café, housed in the building adjacent to the admissions office. The café only had sandwiches and salads, and was clearly priced for parents, but it was our best option, since dining hall food, always questionable, was *especially* suspect during break.

"Are you okay?" Skye narrowed her eyes at me as we stood in line.

"Yeah. Just nervous."

"Briana!" She drew my name out in an exaggerated sigh.

"What?"

"Not nervous. *Excited.* Remember?" With that, she turned away from me and ordered a salad at the counter.

"Right. Excited," I said, pulling my phone from my pocket

and deleting the Tweets I'd written during the audition. It was too risky to have them up.

Skye whirled around and I guiltily clutched my phone.

"Your turn," she said breezily.

After I'd gotten my sandwich, I slid in the seat opposite Skye and wished I'd declined her lunch invite. It was hard to seem normal around Skye in the best of times, and now was definitely not normal.

"So, what did you think?"

"Of the auditions? I guess they were fine. You?"

"I didn't know you were *good*." The way she said it sounded accusatory.

"Is that a compliment?" I joked.

Skye's eyes narrowed, then widened. She gave me a grin. "Of *course* it's a compliment, silly. I just *meant* that *you* were, like, *a surprise*. I bet you'll get the part of the Player Queen."

I raised my eyes to meet her. "I want to be Ophelia."

"Oh, *everyone* wants that part. It's not that great, though. I mean, there's not a *ton* of lines, and then it's going to be weird with Eric. I mean, it's awkward having a love scene with your ex-boyfriend, you know? Unless we get back together. Which I think we will, especially if we're going to be cast opposite each other as love interests. It just makes the play *so* much more *honest*, don't you think?"

I put down my sandwich and pushed my chair back. Skye's self-confidence had made me lose my appetite.

"Sorry, I forgot something back at the dorm," I said, not bothering to wait for her response to my lame excuse. I burst out of the café and into the cold air. But instead of turning toward Rockefeller, I raced back down to the theater.

As I ran, I felt my phone buzz against my hip. I stopped and pulled it out.

Hamlet's Ghost @hamletsghost
Delete all you want, but I enjoyed your earlier Tweets @alleyesonbree. FYI, the *real* show hasn't started yet. #getafrontrowseat

My fingers trembled above the keys. Should I respond? Play dumb? For all I knew, it was one of the other actors, trying to throw me off my game. Not responding would make it seem like they'd rattled me. I had to respond. Finally, I took a deep breath and started typing.

Briana Beland @alleyesonbree
Thanks for the heads up @hamletsghost. No fear, Shakespeare . . . ready for showtime.

I heaved a sigh of relief. Whoever it was, my response sounded confident, cool, and collected.

I perched on a bench in the empty auditorium lobby and pulled out the bagels I'd bought earlier, untouched since this morning. And there, sitting across from Sarah Charonne's unblinking image, I ate my lunch. I wasn't afraid of ghosts.

Or jealous actresses.

CHAPTER 4

Skye Henderson

Eating lunch alone since @alleyesonbree ditched me. Anyone around to keep me company? #riledup #tragedy #auditions

I hurried back to the auditorium, hoping Eric was there as well. I hated how Skye made it sound like she'd already gotten the part. What about the Forsyth kids auditioning for Ophelia? What about me? And where had Eric gone so quickly after O'Dell dismissed us? Could his behavior have less to do with his audition and more to do with performing in front of his ex-girlfriend?

Eric wasn't inside the theater. But Andi was, pacing back and forth onstage. As usual, her cell phone was jammed in her mouth.

"Hey, Andi," I said. Around me, a few kids took their seats. Andi glanced over toward me and squinted, but it seemed like she didn't know where the voice was coming from. Her eyes were large and unfocused.

"Andi?" I said again. "Are you okay?"

She flinched, like she'd been hit with an invisible force, took two staggering steps forward, and then she fell to the ground, her cell phone falling from the stage onto the concrete floor of the auditorium.

"Andi?" I called again, gingerly inching toward her. She lay on her back, making gurgling noises. Foam and blood sputtered from her lips. I dropped to my knees next to her. "Andi, wake up!" I called loudly, wildly hoping she was just being her weird Andi self. That she'd pop up any second and say she was just testing how the stage would react under pressure.

As she continued to writhe, I knew without a shadow of a doubt that she wasn't acting. She was really, really sick. I glanced over my shoulder. The few kids in the auditorium were mostly hunched over their phones and wearing headphones.

"Help!" I called. No one heard me. Andi's breathing was becoming more and more desperate and shallow.

"Yo, let's crush this!" a guy said loudly, bursting into the auditorium from the lobby.

"Help!" I called. "Help!"

The guy stopped in his tracks, horror evident in his face. "Whoa. What's going on?"

"She's sick or . . . something. I don't know."

She groaned loudly, then turned on her side. Every exhale caused flecks of blood to rain down on the stage.

The guy bounded onstage, followed by a few other Forsyth kids. "Don't touch her."

"Hold her down."

"Make sure she doesn't throw up."

People were shouting directions and crowding closer and closer to Andi and me.

"What are you going to do?" It was the boy's voice again. It was loud and abrasive and, all of a sudden, I felt like I was going to faint. I needed to get out. I staggered to my feet, then elbowed my way out of the circle. People crushed from all sides around Andi, until I could barely see her. The otherworldly grunts had turned into shallow gasps of air.

"Guys, we need to call a doctor. Now."

The circle opened, giving me a perfect view of Andi. I gasped. Before, Andi's face had been bright red. Now, it was a bluish-gray hue, the kind of color the sky turned right before a storm.

Camille Chatterjee burst onto the stage. "I called Dr. Booth!" she announced importantly.

"Good," I croaked. I was glad *someone* seemed to be in charge and know what to do.

Just then, the auditorium doors banged open. Everyone swiveled toward the noise as Skye ran into the auditorium.

"Oh my God, oh my God, oh my God," she repeated over and over as she raced toward the stage. She leapt up the stairs and barreled through the crowd, right to the center of the action.

"ANDI. CAN YOU HEAR ME?" Skye yelled in her ear. I flinched at her voice.

"ANDI!" Skye tried again. She grabbed Andi's wrist, roughly pushing up the sleeve of her black sweater. A delicate silver bracelet circled her wrist, its silver plate glinting in the stage lights. "Can someone read that? It might be one of those medical-alert things?"

I tried to step toward Andi, but my feet felt locked in place. I needed to do something. Read her bracelet. Race for the doctor. Anything more than watching Andi helplessly suffer. But no matter how much my brain commanded my body to do *something*, all I could do was watch and stare in horror.

"'If found, return to 15 Red Orchard Road, Hillsboro' . . . I think it's her address," a trembling female voice said.

At that moment, the double doors burst open and Dr. Booth sprinted inside.

"She breathing?" he asked sharply, his gaze resting on mine. I nodded wordlessly.

"She just collapsed onstage. I don't know why. Briana was here first," Skye said breathlessly. The words sounded vaguely accusatory from her lips.

"Hmm." Dr. Booth nodded dispassionately as he scooped Andi into his arms.

Just then, Mr. O'Dell walked in, holding a plastic container from Deli-C that contained half a sandwich. His eyebrows raised at the tableaux in front of him: me and Skye kneeling onstage, everyone else watching us, and Andi's body held in Dr. Booth's arms.

"Is everything all right?" His voice was calm, as though he'd walked in to find the lights off or his desk askew. My heart hammered against my chest.

"Seems this one fainted. They do it all the time here. I'll get her sorted," Dr. Booth said confidently as he walked Andi out of the auditorium. I let myself breathe again. The exhales around me made it clear everyone else had the same reaction. Dr. Booth was right. MacHale students *did* faint all the time. Andi would be fine.

The doors banged shut as Dr. Booth and Andi exited. Skye ran after them, Andi's binder clutched in her arms.

"All right." Mr. O'Dell nodded once before striding to the same spot onstage where Andi's body had been only seconds earlier. “And now that everything’s settled, shall we begin part two of auditions?”

“Yes,” I whispered as I nodded. I couldn’t let anything — even Andi’s accident — throw me off my game. Andi would be fine. It was probably allergies or exhaustion. She’d be *fine.*

Mr. O’Dell nodded. “Good. Let’s begin.”

I walked to my seat in the audience and allowed my body to relax.

“Hey. What did I miss?” Eric slid into the seat next to me.

“Drama,” I said as I watched the corners of Eric’s lips tug into a small smile.

I smiled back. Out of the corner of my eye, I saw Skye walk back into the auditorium. Her gaze landed on us, her face darkening as she took in the scene. I gave her a tiny shrug.

Didn’t she know that, in Shakespeare and in life, all was fair in love and war?

Three hours later, after an audition that seemed more like a boot-camp-style rehearsal, Mr. O’Dell dismissed us. I burst out of the auditorium, finally allowing my brain to slow down and try to process what had happened. The audition was like nothing I’d ever experienced. He’d stop us mid-sentence, ask why we’d read a line a certain way, and ask us to switch parts mid-scene. I’d *heard* him murmur when I’d read certain parts, seen him nod his head.

“What was *that* about?” Eric exploded as soon as we emerged from auditions. It was five o’clock and the weak winter sun had completely set beyond the pond. The gas lamps lining Scholar’s Walk cast a warm glow on the snow-dusted path leading up to the dorms. It was one of those picturesque moments of a typical winter evening that should have been shot for the admissions brochure, but I couldn't appreciate the view. My stomach growled, my temples ached, and I had the same *Is this real life?* sensation I'd had last spring, when I'd stayed up nearly forty-eight hours in a row to finish my MacHale application.

"I know, right?" My voice sounded flat and dispassionate; I'd given everything I could onstage. Eric, however, was furious. His mouth was set in a firm line and there was a whiny edge to his voice.

"Who does this guy think he is? I mean, whatever, they want to add Forsyth. Cool. But then he acts like he's this *god*, embarrassing everyone onstage. . . . It's just low. No, it's not low, it's *disrespectful*. I mean, we all came back early from break, presumably we want to be in this play . . . so why does he act like he's doing us a favor?"

Skye caught up to us. "Eric! You were great!" Her cheeks were red from the cold, and she had a victorious expression in her eyes. I glanced at her suspiciously. Where had her confidence come from?

"Thanks," Eric grunted. "I don't know about that."

"Well, I thought you were *amazing*. Like, *beyond*," Skye continued, still ignoring me.

"I thought so, too, Eric." I wanted to make it clear to Skye that I was here first, that Eric was talking to *me*. But I also hated how down on himself he sounded. After all, Mr. O'Dell hadn't been very hard on him, not like the one Forsyth student he'd reduced to near-tears when he asked if he was trying to do a bad job on purpose. He'd had Eric read for Hamlet, Laertes, and Polonius, stopping him mid-monologue with an "I have what I need." But he'd done that for most everyone else, too.

"Do you think *I* was good?" Skye pressed.

"Sure. You were fine," Eric said in a noncommittal tone.

What about me? I wanted to ask.

"What about Andi?" I finally said.

"What *about* Andi?" Skye shrugged. "She's probably fine. Everyone faints at MacHale. Don't you know that by now?"

She did have a point. I'd seen a few girls faint in gym, and in the dorms, and once during a French presentation. MacHale ran on caffeine and ambition, and a lot of people overdid it. But Andi didn't seem like that type. Still, Skye knew MacHale better than me.

"You know that's not normal, right?" I arched an eyebrow. I didn't want to be talking to Skye at all, but talking about Andi was better than talking about auditions.

"We're not normal. We are la crème de la crème. Unlike these people," she said as a gaggle of Forsyth kids walked by, apparently unaffected by the audition drama. They were laughing loudly, interrupting one another and giggling as they pointed out the sign for the riding trails, the tennis center, and the ceramics workshop. My gaze landed on the blonde girl I'd sat behind during auditions. Her hair fell loose on her polar fleece–covered shoulders, and she laughed easily as a tall, skinny dark-haired guy tried and failed to grab on to the low-hanging branch of an oak tree to the right of the path. I wondered if she'd end up in the cast. If we'd end up as friends. I gave a small smile as she walked by.

"Do you know her?" Eric's gaze followed mine.

"That's Kennedy Clifford," Skye said importantly. "From *Forsyth*. I think O'Dell liked her. And, I mean, I guess she was all right. At least, she was compared to me. I was *terrible*," she said, emphasizing the word as her eyes darted between both of us for compliments.

I glanced over at Eric, pleased that he didn't offer up an automatic compliment. I hated the competitive vibe Skye was giving off. And from the way Eric was looking at the ground and shifting from one foot to the other, I could sense that he didn't like it, either.

"Anyway, good luck, Skye. You were great. Seriously." Eric nodded. Skye's eyes widened as she realized that Eric was politely dismissing her.

Skye turned on her heel and stomped off.

"I guess I should go, too?" I said, the words tumbling out like a question.

"No. Don't. I mean, unless you want to. But I guess I was wondering if you wanted to . . . get dinner or something?" Eric asked shyly.

"Me?" I asked despite myself.

Eric nodded wordlessly, not pulling his gaze from Skye's back. But as soon as Skye was out of our sight line, Eric turned to me. "Sorry you had to witness that." He jerked his chin toward the direction Skye had walked.

"That wasn't bad. I didn't mind."

"It's just the *Am I good? Tell me I'm good. How good was I?*" Eric parroted. "It gets exhausting. And since she and I aren't together or anything, it just seems . . . unnecessary." He jammed his hands in his pockets and turned on his heel, heading in the opposite direction of the dorms. I trailed behind him, my feet crunching through the snow as I tried not to laugh at Eric's comment. Didn't he realize he *was* Hamlet, all moody and insecure? I wished I could point it out, but I couldn't. Not yet. I fast-forwarded a few weeks in my mind, when he and I would be making a mid-rehearsal coffee run and I could tease him for his inability to shrug off his character offstage.

"So, what did you think of auditions? And this isn't a plea for you to tell me I'm good," he said as he hopped the split-rail fence that separated campus from the woods. Several faded PRIVATE PROPERTY: TRESPASSERS WILL BE PROSECUTED signs hung on the trees surrounding the area, but fresh footprints in the snow made it clear that no one took the threats that seriously.

"I'm tired," I said honestly, evading the question. It'd be one thing if we were just talking about auditions. I *knew* I'd done a good job, better than anything I'd ever done in front of Dr. Spidell. Mr. O'Dell may have been some Broadway jerk, but he was also someone who didn't know me as a transfer, as a failed commercial actress, as the daughter of a celebrated MacHale alum who didn't shine half as brightly as her mother. That had been Briana. But now I was Bree, the passionate and fearless actress he'd seen onstage. But then there was the Skye stuff, the Andi illness, the weird Hamlet's Ghost account that had been Tweeting at me. . . . It was a lot to process. And I felt lonely knowing that there was no one I could talk about it with, not really. I couldn't tell Eric about Skye without sounding jealous. I couldn't tell Willow about Eric without risking everyone on campus knowing by tomorrow. I may have been only two feet away from Eric, but the loneliness hadn't gone anywhere.

"I thought you were really great. It's like what I said last night, I really didn't know how talented you were. What else are you hiding, Bree?" Eric asked as his footsteps crunched in the snow.

The fact that I think I'm falling in love with you, I wanted to say. Of course I didn't.

"You were good, too." I said quietly. "But you have to know that, right?"

Eric shrugged and kept looking straight ahead. "I feel like I don't know anything anymore."

In front of me, I saw a yellowish light. I stopped in my tracks. It looked like the eyes I'd thought I'd seen last night.

"You okay?" Eric asked over his shoulder.

I nodded and took a few steps forward. The light disappeared. I squinted, then saw an orange square piece of plastic attached to a tree.

"Oh, they're reflectors!" I said out loud.

"Huh?"

"On the tree. Yesterday, I thought . . . I thought they were eyes."

"Man, you really do have an overactive imagination!"

"Sometimes." I laughed. "Sorry, I'm just not really that woodsy, I guess."

"Well, don't worry. I'm here to protect you." We walked in silence up a small incline. At the top, I saw a church spire in the distance. We were coming into town by the railroad tracks. I did a mental inventory of what was nearby. There was the tiny Italian restaurant that upperclassmen went to on dates, the fancy French fusion restaurant that people only went to when their parents were in town, the sandwich shop . . . nothing quite right for a non-date.

Instead of turning right, though, toward town, Eric turned left.

We walked across the railroad tracks near the Runnymede River and dam. This was the area of town MacHale kids didn't usually visit, the place where the body of Sarah Charonne had been found. It wasn't like we'd been issued a specific warning or had been told to stay away from the actual, non-touristy town of Forsyth, but every single RA, housemistress, advisor, and *Things to Do* handout made it clear that MacHale kids weren't especially welcome over here. Especially now.

"Where are we going?" I asked, walking behind him as the sidewalk ended and both of us walked on the side of the road. A dirty blue pickup truck passed us, its tires rolling into a slushy puddle and sending a spray of water on my dress. My teeth chattered. Just then, Eric turned down a side street, where grimy looking businesses were dotted among one-level homes.

"You don't know anything about MacHale until you've had pizza from here. Way better than Italian Village," he said, naming the place nearby campus that stayed open 24/7 over exam week. Their pizzas tasted like cardboard, but that was made up for by the fact that they delivered straight to your dorm room door.

He walked through a gravel parking lot. Rows of motorcycles were parked against the wood siding. A fluorescent sign, several of its letters burnt out, spelled out THE USTY AX. *The Rusty Ax?* I squinted, noticing the missing letters were a *T* and an *R*. The *Trusty* Ax. That made me feel a little bit better. But not much.

"Is this a bar?" I asked uncertainly. If it was against MacHale rules to go off campus, it was *certainly* not okay for us to be at a bar.

"More like a restaurant. It's fine." He pushed the door open and we were greeted by the scent of stale beer. This *definitely* wasn't what I'd imagined, but I followed him to one of the corner booths and slid in across from him.

A man in the far corner was fiddling with an amplifier, a guitar slung across his back. The air was both pine-scented and smoky due to a brick fireplace on the opposite side of the room.

"Where's Blondie?" A waitress with stringy brown hair asked as she slapped our menus down on our table. She must have meant Skye. I watched Eric's face for a reaction.

"Not here." Eric shrugged. "This is another friend of mine. This is Bree."

"You kids doin' that play?" she asked, noting Eric's crumpled-up copy of *Hamlet*.

"Yup," Eric grunted.

"My daughter went to the auditions for that. You see her? Kennedy?"

That caught my attention. It was hard to believe that this tired-looking woman was related to the blonde girl Skye had pointed out earlier.

"We didn't have time to do introductions," Eric explained.

"Of course you didn't. Well, I hope she did good. I hope you did, too. Now, you kids ordering food?" she asked, her pen poised over her pad.

"Yeah. We'll have the Godfather to split. And mozzarella sticks."

"How'd you find this place?" I asked, choosing the safest-seeming question as our waitress walked away.

"Skye and I used to come here sometimes. When we wanted to get away from the rumor mill."

"Skye wanted to get away from the rumor mill?" I asked skeptically. I couldn't imagine that Skye, who always craved the spotlight, would turn down a chance for people to see and talk about her.

Eric smiled briefly.

"Yeah. I know she can sort of be a diva. But she's also insecure. Sometimes we'd come here so we could . . ." He broke off his thought, as if he'd caught himself revealing something too personal.

"Could do what?" I asked.

A grin flickered on Eric's face. "We actually used to perform here. She had this idea that we'd start a band together. But she didn't want anyone *real* to hear us. So we'd come here. She wanted everyone to be impressed when we performed on campus."

"I guess that makes sense. . . ." I trailed off. I hated hearing about Skye and him, but I also wanted to know everything: How long they'd been together. What *else* they did when no one from MacHale was watching. Who broke up with whom. "Why didn't you ever end up performing?" I asked.

"Because we broke up." Eric shrugged. "Or, rather, because I broke up with her. It's just as well." He turned away from me to watch the guitar player in the corner. The music was something

I didn't recognize, something vaguely country-sounding, all plaintive notes on the guitar and lyrics about lost love.

"Did you guys come here a lot?" I asked.

"Sometimes. It was kind of cool to remember that there's more to life than MacHale. *That's* what MacHale should encourage. Having us get into town and meet people. Not bringing all of the Forsyth kids on campus. I mean, I think it's great that they're doing the play, I just hate how the administration is turning everything into such a big deal. I mean, it's not like the MacHale campus is that special. I think this place is much more interesting," Eric said, gesturing to a row of guitars hanging on the wall above the corner stage.

I imagined Skye and Eric on the tiny stage. Skye singing while Eric's arms were wrapped around her waist. The two of them entirely in their own world, oblivious to the fact the Forsyth locals were watching them.

I didn't want to think about it anymore, so I turned my attention back to Eric. "Seriously, though, why were you so upset about auditions? You did great. You *know* you did great."

"I don't like when people ask you to prove yourself, you know? I think that's actually why things ended between Skye and me. I felt like she was always wanting me to act like the perfect boyfriend or whatever."

"But isn't the whole point of acting to *not* be yourself?" I asked.

"No, not really." Eric shook his head. "I mean, I know I'm playing a character. I know that I need to follow whatever direction I'm given. But I don't want someone to try to manipulate me into being scared, or nervous, or whatever. I don't like that whole *Let's put you to a test* thing that O'Dell did. It wasn't necessary. Don't you think?"

"I guess so," I agreed. But I'd felt the opposite. I'd loved the challenge, and I still felt the audition adrenaline running through my veins. I only wished that Eric would snap out of his mood.

"But you *know* you're Hamlet. You were the best," I said as the waitress placed a pizza in between us. Steam wafted from the cheese, curling around the eggplant, meatball slices, and pepperoni. My stomach growled.

"You're just saying that so I give you the biggest slice, right?" Eric asked as he slid a large piece onto my plate.

"Exactly," I joked.

My phone buzzed.

Tristan Schuler

Looking for @alleyesonbree for a post #audition #gossipsession tout de suite. Where are you?

"Ugh," I whispered under my breath.

"What?"

"Tristan."

"Let me guess. He's starting a rumor about us hanging out together. Am I right?"

I shook my head, relieved I was staring down at the screen so Eric wouldn't see me blush. "He's just asking about auditions."

My thoughts turned back to the Hamlet's Ghost Tweets. *Of course* that had been him. Who else could it have been?

"Well, just so you know, I wouldn't be mad if he *did* start a rumor about you and me."

I turned away quickly, aware that my cheeks were burning. I was afraid to glance up and look in Eric's eyes and see the inevitable glint of laughter. After all, he had to be kidding.

But what if he wasn't kidding?

I had no idea how to respond, so I stalled for time thinking of a semi-decent Tweet to Tristan.

> **Briana Beland** @alleyesonbree
> Just keeping an eye on the locals. Be back soon, and be good.

I shoved my phone away. Eric's shoulders had relaxed and he was nodding his head to the music. He turned toward me, as though he'd sensed me staring, then smiled. *He likes me.* The thought flitted through my brain before my self-defense mechanisms had time to squash it. Could *that* be what his comment meant? Why he kept talking about his breakup with Skye? I glanced around the restaurant. The four walls were covered with faded posters advertising ancient music acts. Was this going to become *our* place? I tried to imagine a few weeks down the line, settling into the cracked-red-vinyl booth and joking about some ridiculous thing that happened in rehearsal. My stomach flipped in anticipation. Whatever the future held, I couldn't wait.

"Sorry I was so emo before," Eric said with a sigh. "The audition was just a lot different than I thought it'd be."

"Yeah. I mean, I guess I don't have anything to compare it to," I said uncertainly.

"You're kind of lucky. You get used to things being done a certain way. I don't deal well with change. You're pretty brave to just come here, not knowing anyone."

"I don't think I'm brave." I laughed, to try to make it sound like a joke. I wanted to see what he saw, because whenever I saw myself in the mirror, all I saw was a girl desperately trying to figure out who she was: Was she the artsy roomie or the peppy scene partner? The been-there-done-that bored kid in the back of the auditorium or the one who channeled everything she had and blew herself away on stage?

A shadow crossed our table.

"We've already ordered." Eric barely looked up.

But I did. I recognized the shock of red hair and freckle-covered face looming above us. "You're —"

"The kid who was kicked out. You want to laugh about it, too?" the guy asked defensively. My stomach twisted in sympathy. Mr. O'Dell had seen Tristan and me joking with each other. If he'd wanted to, he could have kicked me out as well.

"That's rough, man," Eric said. "Can I get another soda?"

"Eric!" I hissed, almost kicking him under the table. He'd seemed so empathetic, but some switch had flipped and now he was acting like a typical spoiled MacHale kid. But my surprise and discomfort washed away as a smirk formed on the Forsyth kid's face.

"Sure thing. You need anything?" His gaze landed on me. I shook my head and looked down, but I could still sense him staring. "Bree?"

My head jerked up, as though I were called on unprepared in French class. "Me?"

The guy snickered. "Yes, you."

I nodded. "Yeah. Bree. Well, Briana. Briana Beland."

"Lots of options, then. Good. I like a girl with some variety." He turned and sauntered toward the kitchen. Once he was out of earshot, Eric leaned in toward me.

"Do you know him?"

I shook my head. "Just at the audition."

I fiddled with my napkin, feeling vaguely guilty, even though I shouldn't. The red-haired guy hadn't been flirting. Eric and I weren't together.

"Seems pretty friendly." There was an edge to Eric's voice.

"Yup." An uncomfortable silence fell between us.

"Wait." Eric leaned toward me. "Look over by the bar."

Sitting by himself, midway down the polished oak bar in the front of the restaurant was a guy wearing a button-down denim shirt and a fedora, clearly out of place amid the burly flannel shirt-clad loggers surrounding him.

"Is that O'Dell?" he whispered.

"Is it?" I asked, my face reddening. I felt as though we'd been caught — or that we'd caught him.

Eric nodded wordlessly. Part of me wanted to go over to him, introduce myself, ask if he needed me to perform another monologue. Eric was also staring at Mr. O'Dell intently.

"Should we introduce ourselves?" I whispered.

As though he'd heard us, Mr. O'Dell's gaze snapped up, and I immediately looked away. From the grubby window, I could just make out the outline of the MacHale dorms, their silhouettes dark and ominous in the moonlit evening. The guitar had stopped, I realized, and Led Zeppelin played from the jukebox.

"He's gone." Something had shifted in the moments since we'd seen Mr. O'Dell, and now Eric was fidgeting with his coat. "We should still head out. I've got Millard as my house master and he's strict about curfew." A small smile played on Eric's face. "Sorry. I feel like you must think I'm so lame. Auditions aren't my thing. And now I can't get my mind off them. Sorry, I'm just not good company right now."

"Well, you're a good pizza orderer, so I guess I'll forgive you." I pushed my own plate away, even though I'd barely managed a few bites.

The waitress dropped the check between us.

"We can split it," I said quickly as I fumbled for my wallet.

"Nah, you put up with me. I've got it." Eric fished in his pocket for cash.

My phone buzzed and I jumped. Had someone texted me? Instead, it was a new Tweet.

> **Hamlet's Ghost** @hamletsghost
> It seems like @alleyesonbree may be on another audition . . . to be or not to be Eric's girlfriend? I'll be watching.

"Oh my God, Tristan," I groaned. I rolled my eyes and shoved the phone toward Eric. "What do you think?" I asked. "It has to be him, right?"

"Probably." He tilted his head to the side. "But it's a little bit insulting how upset you're getting about the implication that we're together."

"I'm not!" I protested, mortified.

Eric's eyes danced with laughter. "Right. Whatever you say.

And whatever *Tristan* says. I'm done with rumors. If people want to talk about us, who cares?"

My heart soared at the word *us*. I suddenly wanted to hug Tristan. Yes, he was a weird busybody who clearly had spoken to *someone* who'd seen us leave together, but Eric's reaction to the Tweet was more than I ever could have wanted. He liked me. Or, rather, he didn't care whether people had seen us together. But the details didn't matter. What mattered was that Eric's mood seemed to have lifted. I was hoping he'd change his mind and want to stay at the restaurant longer, when the door swung open and a posse of Forsyth kids from the audition walked in, immediately taking over a large table on the opposite side of the room.

"Let's go." Eric nodded.

"Sure." I tried to conceal my disappointment. I hurried after him as we left the restaurant, our footsteps crunching on the gravel pavement as we fell into step toward campus.

Eric walked quickly, and I had to lengthen my stride to keep up with him. The air felt heavy, and clouds covered the moon. I kept thinking back to the eyes in the woods that I'd seen the night before. During the day, they'd been as inconsequential as an image in a dream. But now they felt very real. I squinted, trying to conjure the same image. Maybe it had been a trick of the light, or the effect of my contact lens folding against itself in my eye. I took a step and stumbled, tumbling down onto my knees with a thud.

"Ow!" I yelped as my un-mittened hands plunged into the snow, submerging my iPhone. I blinked, then rubbed my eyes. My vision was blurry. Clearly, one of my contacts had fallen out during the fall.

I scrambled to my feet. My knee hurt and my hands felt raw from the cold.

"You okay?" I felt Eric's strong hand on my shoulder.

"I lost my phone. And my contact," I said in a small voice.

"I need to keep my eye on you, huh? Probably a hand, too." Eric combed through the snow as I wiped my face with my gloved hand. I wasn't crying, but I was close. My knee stung, but it was my pride that was hurt. Whenever things started going well with us, I felt like my overactive imagination had to ruin it. Now he'd *definitely* think I was a bizarre weirdo.

"Found the phone. Think the contact is lost, though." Eric stood up and wiped my phone on his gloved hand, but the screen looked dark and wet in the moonlight. "Thanks."

"Are *you* okay?" Eric reached over and brushed snow off my shoulder.

I nodded. "Nothing's broken." I pushed the center button on my phone only to stare back at a blank screen. "Not so sure about this, though."

Eric pulled it from my hand to examine it. "Just put it in a bowl of rice. It works. I dropped my phone down the toilet like five times last year."

"I'll give it a shot," I said uncertainly, trying to ignore the waves of pain radiating from my knee. "What did I trip on, anyway?" I looked down at the ground below. Instead of a rock or log, there was a smooth slate slab half covered with snow beneath my feet.

I bent over and brushed the snow from the granite surface. The date 1823 came into view, etched and faded into the granite. I shivered as I ran my finger along the numbers. "Is this . . ."

"A tombstone," Eric finished.

"Augh!" I shrieked and pulled my hand back as though I'd touched the corpse itself.

"Yeah, this used to be a graveyard back in the nineteenth century. Pretty much *any* large area of land up here has a graveyard in it. They won't hurt you, though. Can you walk?" Eric held out a hand toward me.

"I think I'm okay," I said, but I still grabbed his hand as we picked our way to the split-rail fence and he helped me over and back onto campus.

He paused when we reached the path to the dorms. Underneath the dusting of snow, tiny metallic pieces stuck in the concrete sparkled in the gas-lamp light. My shoulders relaxed. Everything was *fine*. But I still felt uneasy. How was there a graveyard right next to campus?

"What are you going to do as soon as you get back to your room?" he asked, in a voice that made it sound like he already knew the answer.

"Um . . ." I trailed off guiltily. Clearly, I was going to obsessively check Twitter and pump Willow for information about what happened between Skye and Eric. Then I remembered. My phone.

"Putting my phone in rice," I said triumphantly.

"Good answer," Eric said. "It was fun hanging out. Good night and good luck." He gave me a mock salute and headed down the walkway.

I watched as he walked out of sight, startling when the bell at the top of Taylor Hall chimed seven o'clock. I turned and raced down the path to Rockefeller. My heart hammered in rhythm to the throbbing pain in my knee. The fall had shaken me. By Eric's side, I'd felt braver, bolder, better. That feeling had been shattered as soon as my knees hit the cold, wet ground. It was a reminder how even — *especially* — when everything seemed to be going well, it was all too easy to slip and fall.

You're fine, I thought to myself as I swiped into Rockefeller and breathed heavily in the lobby. I'd had a good audition. I'd successfully flirted with Eric. I was better than fine. Sure, my boots were soaking wet and my stockings had ripped during the fall. A scrape oozed blood. But none of that mattered.

In the communal kitchen, I found an ancient box of instant rice, probably left there from a decade earlier, and dumped it in a bowl, then submerged my phone.

"Ms. Beland?"

I stifled a yelp. Maybe I wasn't as fine as I thought.

"It's just me, dear." Ms. Robinette stood there with a pot of tea in one hand and a plastic container of cookies in the other. "I wanted to invite everyone for tea in the common room. A house meeting, if you will. Can you spread the word?"

I glanced down, amazed at how Ms. Robinette was oblivious to my bleeding knee and my soaked feet. And then I noticed her eyes were red-rimmed and her skin was blotchy.

"Is everything all right?" I asked. She was wearing her night-gown with a robe over it. Her hair was in curlers and she wasn't wearing makeup. She was *always* fully dressed for a house meeting.

Ms. Robinette sighed. "Just get everyone, please. As soon as possible."

"Of course," I agreed. She probably wanted to remind us not to have guests in the dorms or keep our straightening irons plugged in when we weren't in our rooms. I grabbed the bowl with my phone and hurried away, quickly allowing the image of Ms. Robinette in her nightgown to be replaced by an image of Eric in his shorts. I smiled. Much better.

CHAPTER 5

Zach Mathis

Hey @alleyesonbree, we met at the Trusty Ax earlier. Wanna do coffee and talk theater sometime? Seems I've got a lot of free time on my hands. . . .

I walked into the common room, which smelled like nail polish remover, body lotion, and stale french fries — the familiar scent of dorm living. The only difference was how few girls were scattered around the room. Normally, every inch of floor space was taken. Today, the unoccupied chairs scattered around the cavernous space made the room look even bigger than it normally was.

I scanned the room, taking note of who was here for Winterm. Gina Maestre, a freshman back early to work on her sculpture project, was flipping through a magazine. Allison Ellis and Elizabeth Curtis, two student government seniors, were already in their pajamas and watching something on Allison's iPad. Laura Russo, still wearing her running clothes, her face red from the cold and from her nightly ten-mile run, sat in the corner, stretching. Willow was perched on the window seat in a vintage ivory silk slip and an oversize fedora, taking artsy Instagram selfies.

I boldly plopped down next to Willow. Normally, I'd wait to be invited, but today had made it clear that something had changed.

"Yo!" Willow took one more photo. I blinked at the flash. She grinned. "So, I heard you and Eric are an item?"

I furrowed my brow. "Not exactly."

"Aha!" Willow gave me a sly look. "So there *is* something going on."

"We went to dinner. How do you know . . . ?"

"I got a text from Tristan. He knows everything." She rolled her eyes good-naturedly.

"I gathered that. And get this: He made up a fake Twitter account to mess with me. Does he normally do stuff like that?"

"Normal?" Willow huffed. "There is no such thing as normal when it comes to Tristan."

"Still, can I show you? It's just weird," I said, aware as the words left my mouth that I was acting like Skye, pretending to be annoyed by the spotlight when I secretly craved it.

"Ugh, are you seriously trying to suck me into Twitter? You can't do it. I won't let you. I only do Instagram. Photos don't lie."

"Forget about it," I said, suddenly embarrassed that I'd let fake Tweets from an imaginary ghost freak me out. "So how was your day?"

"It was good!" She narrowed her eyes at me. "Actually, is that my dress?"

Oops. I tugged nervously at the hem. "Um . . ."

"It looks great on you! I told you that you could borrow my stuff whenever you want! Did you wear it to the auditions? How'd they go?"

"They were . . . weird." I tried to figure out where to begin. I couldn't believe it was still the same day. But before I could begin, Ms. Robinette strode into the lobby. She'd changed from her nightgown into her typical black pants and white button-down shirt, which made her look like a waitress. Or a penguin. I wished I could Tweet that observation. Tristan would have laughed.

"Girls?" Ms. Robinette asked soberly. "I need your *full* attention. *Ladies?*" She glanced meaningfully at Allison and Elizabeth, who guiltily snapped their heads up from their iPad.

"This isn't easy to say, but . . . there's been an accident on campus today. Andrea Schaefer has passed away." Ms. Robinette's lower lip trembled. Laura gasped.

"She *died*?" a senior asked from the back of the room.

Ms. Robinette nodded. "It's a terrible tragedy."

My stomach twisted. I thought of Andi's agonized breathing onstage, the slow trickle of blood from the corner of her mouth. "I was there," I croaked, unaware I'd spoken until I realized that everyone in the room was staring at me. "At the audition. I saw her . . ."

"I am *so sorry* you had to witness that, Briana, darling," Ms. Robinette said, shaking her head. "Of course if you need to talk to anyone, my door is always open."

"What happened?" a girl asked me, her eyes wide with a strange mixture of horror and excitement.

"She poisoned herself," Ms. Robinette said briskly before I had time to respond.

What? "No," I started to say. "That's not what happened . . ." but my voice trailed off as the room broke into a flurry of whispers.

Ms. Robinette cleared her throat and looked stern. "It seems she may have accidentally ingested battery acid from her phone, which ended up poisoning her."

Two tiny freshman girls in matching velour sweatpants and flimsy MacHale camisoles burst into giggles.

Ms. Robinette glared at them. "It's not funny. It's a tragedy. Though I know you're likely reacting to the shock of the news. That's why psychological services will be open all day tomorrow, for anyone who might need to talk. In the meantime, I ask that you respect the privacy of Andrea's parents and *not* discuss this tragedy on social media, or with anyone outside the MacHale community who may want to report on this story."

Willow nodded somberly. I glanced down at my dead phone. How could a *phone* be deadly? I thought back to the way Tristan and I had laughed at her, the way she couldn't keep the phone out of her mouth.

Pockets of conversation sprang up around me, but I didn't want to engage with anyone. It was as if the weird feelings I'd sensed all day had collected together to form a tsunami that had broken on top of me, engulfing me in a tangle of confusion and exhaustion.

"One more thing, ladies?" Our focus snapped back to Ms. Robinette, who rewarded us with a bright smile. "I made tea. Please feel free to help yourselves."

Without waiting for an answer, she shuffled toward the kitchen. No one else had left the room. I didn't want to be here, but I also didn't want to be the first to leave. I turned toward Willow, who was busy choosing a filter for the selfie she'd taken just moments before Ms. Robinette's announcement. It struck me as a strange thing to do moments after learning that one of our classmates had died, but Willow was being so friendly to me, it didn't seem like a good time to start being judgmental.

"Are you okay?" I whispered hoarsely, even though it was

obvious she was. What I needed, I realized, was for someone to ask me the same question.

Willow nodded. "I didn't know her very well. I mean, we were in a sculpture class together. . . ." She trailed off. "But, I mean, maybe it's for the best."

I blinked hard, trying to suss out Willow's facial expression. But with only one contact, everything was blurry, lending an even more bizarre cast to the scene that had just unfolded. Willow sounded so callous. Had she said what I'd thought she'd said?

"What do you mean?"

"I mean, like, survival of the fittest or whatever. If she couldn't keep herself from eating her phone, then maybe she *wasn't* meant for this world, you know?" Willow blithely shrugged her shoulders. Near her, a few senior girls who'd overheard her nodded in agreement.

"But don't you think it's weird to just *swallow* your cell phone battery? I mean, who does that?" I pressed. Something about the death didn't seem right. Of course, I'd seen her in the auditorium, flailing and desperate. But, then again, I'd also seen her spend the entire morning of the audition with the corner of her phone firmly placed between her two canine teeth.

"Andi does!" One of the seniors laughed.

"No, listen!" I said sharply.

The senior narrowed her eyes at me. "Yes?"

"I'm just saying . . . do you think someone could have poisoned her?" I knew right away it wasn't the right thing to say aloud. It made me sound naïve and paranoid. Yet I couldn't shake the uneasy feeling tugging at the edges of my shock.

Willow snorted in laughter. "No offense, but Andi's not exactly important enough to poison."

I stifled a shiver. Apparently, at MacHale, you had to be someone even to be worthy of being murdered.

"Are you okay? You look weird," Willow said.

Just then, Ms. Robinette came back in with a tray laden with mugs of tea. I grabbed one and took a few deep sips, letting the warmth wash over me. Willow turned back to Instagram, the two seniors slipped into a conversation about internships, and for what felt like the first time that day, I was invisible again. Yet this time, I welcomed the anonymity. I took that chance to hurry back to our room, where I turned on the lights and got under the covers. It was barely after eight, but I was exhausted.

"Rest in peace, Andi," I whispered, right before I closed my eyes and allowed sleep to overtake me.

When I woke up early the next morning, Willow was sound asleep in the bed across from mine. I squinted, trying to get the contact in my right eye to fall into place. I'd fallen asleep with it in and it was now stuck to my eyeball, reminding me of the ancient wadded-up pieces of gum stuck for eternity on the hallway walls. I blinked several times to try to eek moisture from my tear ducts, and it was only when a tear began to form that all the events from yesterday came slamming back into my brain.

Auditions. Eric. Hamlet's Ghost. Andi. Dead.

Each thought was followed by another more terrible event, creating an avalanche of emotion that caused *real* tears to leak out of my eyes.

Andi was dead. It was a fact, not a dream, but it seemed even less real than the creepy eyes I'd seen in the woods a few nights back or the very real fear I had of Sarah Charonne's ghost. I reached under my pillow for my phone. Where was my phone? Then, I turned and saw it on the floor, sticking up from a bowl of rice like a lopsided candle on a birthday cake.

I crossed the room and opened my laptop. I typed *twi* into the address bar and pressed RETURN as *twitter.com* auto-filled into the blank space.

A window popped up.

Browser not connected to the Internet.

My stomach sank.

Of course it wasn't. The Internet went out almost weekly in Rockefeller, and the IT department never gave a good reason. Personally, I thought Ms. Robinette had something to do with it. She knew everyone used their laptops after lights-out, and she took sleep very seriously. Normally, no one minded, since they could always use their phones for any late-night Facebook stalking or Snapchatting. But with both out of commission, I was lost. Untethered.

Not knowing what else to do, I swung my legs out of bed, pulling a sweatshirt over my tank top and not bothering to change out of my pajama pants. I didn't care what I looked like right now; who would possibly be awake and functional on campus this early? I wasn't even sure if the dining hall would be open, but I decided to test my luck. The dining hall had two communal computers that were hardly ever used, which would at least allow me *some* contact with the outside world.

My breath formed white clouds of smoke with each exhale. Whatever adrenaline I'd had yesterday had disappeared, replaced by the far more familiar waves of anxiety that radiated from my brain to my body.

The sounds of heavy breathing made me turn from my spot at the dining hall entrance. Coming up from the wooded path was a man wearing a black fleece hat, running pants, and a purple fleece pullover. I squinted to see if I recognized him. I could see goldish curls springing from underneath the hat.

"Ophelia!"

What had he called me?

I whirled around. "Mr. O'Dell?" The squeak in my voice gave away any attempt at being casual. I couldn't tell how old he was. I couldn't tell whether or not he was attractive. I couldn't tell what made him interesting — yesterday, it had been his New York *artiste* leather ensemble, so out of place in the Maine woods. But today he was wearing the same thing Mr. Ervin, the gym teacher, wore to class, and I never felt the urge to stare at Coach Ervin. This, I realized, was what presence was. It was having an aura that made it impossible for anyone to look away.

"Good morning." Mr. O'Dell stopped and stamped his feet theatrically on the ground. "Trying to get some exercise in this tundra is harder than getting backers for an indie short film, don't you think?" he asked, as if he knew what he was talking about. He was barely breathing heavily. Meanwhile, my breath was coming in short bursts, and sweat was running down the back of my neck. How could I listen to him when he'd called me *Ophelia*?

"I had fun at the auditions yesterday!" I blurted, to fill the silence. "I mean, until Andi's accident." I froze, horrified by how callous I sounded. "Sorry, it's early, and I didn't sleep much," I babbled, trying to save myself. Finally, I mashed my lips together and silently prayed he wouldn't judge me.

His eyes crinkled.

"I am so sorry I just sounded like an idiot," I said.

I clapped my hand over my mouth. *What* was I doing?

Mr. O'Dell smiled tightly. "You had fun at the auditions. Well, that's something I don't hear often. You're interesting, Ms. . . . ?"

"Beland. Briana Beland. But some people are calling me Bree now. I mean, some people have always called me Bree, but I've never used it as an official name, like, with teachers. But since I'm new here this year, I figured that I'd just call myself Bree. Or Ophelia!" I babbled, realizing as I spoke that *interesting* was probably interchangeable with *insane*. But it was too late to change anything.

"Bree. I didn't remember your name, but I remembered your performance. The Ophelia monologue."

"Thank you, sir!" I said brightly, realizing as the words left my lips that he'd said he *remembered* it, not that he liked it.

"Well, I'll see you soon." He pulled his earbuds from his pocket.

"Wait!"

"Yes?" He cocked his head.

I took a deep breath. He already had to think I was a sociopath. I didn't have anything to lose. "When are you going to post the cast list?" I asked. My heart thumped wildly in my chest.

"Why? Are you nervous?"

"A little," I confessed.

"I'm planning to post the cast list quite soon. By three p.m. at the latest. Can you tell the others? Thank you."

Before I could respond, he popped in his earbuds and took off down the jogging path. "Wait!" I called. My phone was still dead. I didn't *know* the others. What was I supposed to do?

But he didn't turn around.

"Hold up!" I called again. But his form only retreated into the distance.

I made a split-second decision and headed to Burnside.

Burnside was the upperclassmen boys' dorm, named after the poet Robert Burns and, as every tour guide reminded prospective students, a proud reminder of MacHale's Scottish heritage. It was also the farthest from the center of campus, all the way on the other side of the pond.

I was weighing my options on the steps when the door creaked open. Chad-or-Tad wandered out in workout gear and a MACHALE LACROSSE cap, pulled down so low on his forehead I couldn't even see his eyebrows to verify his identity.

"Yo." He blinked at me.

"Hey. Is Tristan around?" I tried to sound casual.

"Yeah. He's around." Chad-or-Tad nodded.

"Where?" I asked.

"Oh, you want to see him? He's my roommate."

"Which *room*?" I asked, trying to stay patient. That was the thing I was learning about MacHale: Everyone expected you to *know* things — from how to sneak out of the dorms to which teachers only gave open-book exams to how Sarah Charonne had died. But no one ever told you how they knew this stuff.

"Oh, right. Thirty-six."

"Thanks." I walked through the open door as the scent of cologne and dirty socks assaulted my nose, one hundred times more offensive than the Rockefeller common room, even during finals week. No wonder all the guys tried to sneak into the girls' dorm instead of vice versa. While the Rockefeller hallways were covered with photos, posters, and signs for pep rallies and birthdays, the Burnside walls were blank, and the paint was chipping. The hallway was narrower than Rockefeller, and I noticed a few Italian Village boxes seeping grease in the corner.

40, 39 . . . Finally, I reached room 36. I paused for a second before I gently rapped on the door.

Nothing.

I knocked again, louder this time.

"Seriously? How many times have I tried to tell you to just put your running stuff out the night before so you don't forget anything?" a muffled voice whined on the other side of the door.

I shifted from one foot to the other. Maybe this hadn't been a good idea. But just as I was about to leave, the door inched open. Tristan blinked up at me a few times, holding the doorframe as if it was the only thing keeping him from collapsing onto the floor. His black hair was matted on one side and spiky on the other, and his baggy flannel pajama pants and oversize sweatshirt made him look way younger than he did when he was in full hipster wear.

"Sorry. It's early. I'll go," I said quickly, turning my eyes to the floor.

"No, come in." He swung the door open. "Sorry to yell at you. I thought you were Tad. He always forgets something. He's like a golden retriever, always coming back to fetch. Only he drools more."

"That's funny," I said, too keyed up to actually laugh. I stepped inside. The room itself was similar to our Rockefeller room, but the south-facing windows had a view to the woods rather than the pond. A tree stood in one corner of the room, its leaves drooping. The other side of the room looked like an earthquake had exploded. Bow ties littered the floor, half-crushed soda cans were everywhere, and a piece of string cheese was placed carefully across the psych textbook on the desk like a bookmark.

"I live in *this* part, clearly," Tristan clarified. "It's truly tragic. My roommate lives like a pig and drags us all down in the mud. Positively Shakespearean. And this is his mess from December. He didn't clean before he left, and *I'm* not touching it. He keeps saying he will. But he doesn't. Instead, he'll clean after he goes for a run. Or after he hangs out with Willow. Or after he pretends to go for a run but really goes to hang out with Willow. Or after he *auditions* for the play, so he can hang out with Willow when she's the costume designer. In case you didn't realize, my roommate is obsessed with your roommate. But he won't *do* anything about it."

"I kind of gathered they liked each other. But Willow and I aren't really friends." I shrugged. "I mean, we're *friends*, but not . . . you know."

Tristan smiled knowingly. "Nice Ice. It's a MacHale specialty, along with ceramics, sending alumni to premier liberal arts colleges, and springing bombshells on current students. Friendly on the surface but never really getting close. People don't want to break The Bubble. The Bubble being MacHale, of course."

"Yup." *Nice Ice. The Bubble.* I tried to file away the terms in my mind for later. I felt like I needed a glossary after talking with Tristan. I knew he had just woken up, but he was already speaking in sharp sound bites. Meanwhile, I wasn't entirely confident I was speaking English.

"So, Andi bit it. Let's discuss." Tristan perched on the edge of the bed and arched an eyebrow up at me.

"Um, that's not really what I was here to . . . discuss."

"Good." Tristan clapped his hands together. "So *boring*. I mean, I feel sad for the girl. It sucks. Or . . . bites, I guess. But it also *really* makes things depressing. And January is already dismal. So, let's talk something happier. Like, say, you and Eric."

"Well, first I need a favor. The cast list is supposed to be up by three, and Mr. O'Dell wants to spread the word. Think Hamlet's Ghost can do it?" I asked.

"I'm not sure about Hamlet's Ghost, but I can. Hold on." He pulled his phone from the pocket of his pajamas and quickly typed. He paused, frowned, typed more, then smiled. "Done. Now. Let's get to the good stuff."

"Well . . ." I trailed off, unsure where to begin. Part of me wanted to tell him everything about Eric. And part of me still didn't trust him.

"Wait!" Tristan leapt up from his bed so quickly that I jumped. "We *must* have caffeine if we're going to have a conversation. Don't you agree, Bree?" Tristan asked as though I had any say in the matter. I nodded as Tristan rummaged through his closet, finally revealing what looked like a well-stocked hotel minibar. A dual coffee machine and espresso maker sat on a shelf next to a collection of various coffee flavors.

"Coffee?" He turned toward me expectantly.

"Sure?" It was a question more than a response. I perched on the edge of the bed and Tristan eyed me reproachfully.

"Bree-an-a," he said, emphasizing each syllable. "I would have thought you'd known better."

"What?" I sprang to my feet.

"No outside clothes on the comforter!"

"Sorry!" I stood up to leave.

"I *suppose* it will be all right." Tristan handed me a steaming cup of coffee. "Sit. No one knows that rule. Or at least, no one follows it but me. Maybe I'm the one who's germophobic. So where have you been? Also, I *know* we're supposed to talk about happy things, but can I just tell you something *tragic* about the Andi situation? Dr. Conger wants me to run a story in the paper about the dangers of cell phones. As if all of us are just chewing on everything. Seriously?" Tristan rolled his eyes.

"Sounds rough." I hated how everyone was making fun of Andi's death. Not like I was any better. I was just better at keeping my thoughts to myself. At least I was for now.

"You have no idea. We go to one of the best boarding schools in the country and we need a reminder to not eat *batteries*? If you ask me, we're better off without her. Anyway, that's enough of my drama. I can't even bear to talk about it anymore; the more seconds I spend discussing the situation, the more brain cells I feel dying. So let's talk about you. What's going on?" Tristan asked expectantly.

I briefly told him about my run-in with Skye, followed by my conversation with Mr. O'Dell.

"So, Skye is mad at you. Why do you care? Don't you not really like her?"

I shrugged. "Well, I want to be nice."

Tristan made a retching sound.

"What?" I asked.

" 'I want to be *nice.'* That's not very aspirational, All Eyes on Bree," he chided, as though I were a block-stealing kindergartener and he was a benevolent babysitter. "You may not want to admit it, but I can see it. You want to be a star. Actually, no." He shook his head. "You believe you *are* a star. As you should. Any other attitude is giving up."

I shifted uneasily in my chair. I didn't like the way Tristan was staring at me, as though he knew me better than I knew myself. When we were Tweeting back and forth, reacting to the audition drama swirling around us, I knew exactly what I wanted to say. But when we were face-to-face, I felt shy. Whenever he laughed, I wondered if it was *at* me. It felt more genuine when it was in Tweet form. From his account. I took a deep breath. I was ready to confront him.

"So, what's the deal with that Hamlet's Ghost thing?"

"Huh?" Tristan cocked his head.

"That account . . . on Twitter. It was Tweeting about stuff that happened yesterday. I was pretty freaked out when I realized it sort of predicted Andi's accident."

Tristan shook his head. "*No comprende.* What are you talking about?"

"You just Tweeted from it!"

Tristan shook his head. "No I didn't. See?" He shoved his phone under my nose.

Tristan Schuler

Who's ready for drama? Hamlet cast list posted at 3pm today. I'll bring tissues, you bring yourselves!

"But I thought . . ." I scrolled halfway down until I found a Hamlet's Ghost Retweet. I clicked on the avatar.

The profile was empty, and it had no followers. But the photo had been changed. Instead of the default egg shape, it was a photo of a full moon. I shivered as I read its latest Tweet, posted late last night.

> **Hamlet's Ghost** @hamletsghost
> Double, double, toil and trouble . . . Wrong play, but when #forsyth and #machale mix, that's what's I expect to be on the way.

"That's not you?" I asked dubiously, holding the phone up toward him.

"Do I *seem* like I'd thrive on anonymity?" Tristan placed his hand on his hips and pouted. "Trust me, I only Tweet as myself. But it seems like Hamlet's Ghost cares a lot about gossip. Which brings us back to the question I had in the first place: What is going on between you and Eric?"

My cheeks turned hot. "Nothing. I mean, we just grabbed food."

"Interesting." A half smile appeared on Tristan's face.

"Don't tell anyone, okay?"

"Why not?" Tristan asked. "You're single, he's single. . . . It's perfect. And it's not like people don't *know* already. Dude, you've got a ghost talking about it. I'd say the secret's out. And adding more gossip only adds more heat. Let me write about you guys, and I'm doing *you* a favor. Please? I need scandal, not public service announcements!" Tristan stuck his lower lip out at me.

"Thanks. But I'd rather everything just sort of go back on the DL. I mean, Eric did just break up with Skye. . . . And then there's the whole cast list coming out. . . . It just seems complicated." As I spoke, I wondered how well Eric and Tristan really knew each other. They seemed to be in the same artistic and leadership orbit, but I couldn't imagine Eric having the patience to deal with Tristan's teasing and almost aggressive fact-gathering.

"Do you always do that?" Tristan asked.

"Do what?"

"Make excuses for going after what you want. It's like you stop yourself. If you want Eric, you should go after Eric. You shouldn't worry about Skye. Or the play. I mean, what do they have to do with you and Eric? You've got to seize the day."

"Easier said than done," I muttered. "So, what were your thoughts on the auditions, anyway?" I asked to change the subject.

"What did I think about auditions before I got *unceremoniously* kicked out, do you mean? I hate to ask, but *does he know who I am*? I mean, I'm not just some random townie. And on that note, I think it's pretty lame that they're combining Forsyth and MacHale, for one. It just seems . . . messy," he said, the emphasis on the word *messy* making it clear that it was one of the worst insults he could bestow on something.

"Really?" I couldn't figure out why everyone was so against the Forsyth kids being part of the play.

Tristan nodded. "We've always done our own thing. And they should do theirs. I mean, I didn't end break early to hang out with townies."

"I thought no one came to MacHale to *hang out*. I thought they came here to expand their horizons and pad their college applications," I joked.

Tristan rewarded me with a smile. "Well, that goes without saying, obviously. But we're different than them. And MacHale people don't play well with others. The longer you stay here, the more you'll see it."

"Oh, I've already seen it." I waited for Tristan to ask why, so I could probe into why people were treating Andi's death like a joke. But Tristan didn't take the bait. Instead, he just yawned theatrically.

"It's early. Talk to me at noon when I'm more coherent. I think a bunch of us are going to town. You coming?"

"I guess so," I said uncertainly. I'd never met anyone harder to read than Tristan. "If I'm invited."

"You are. As of now, you're one of us. I've decided."

"Is there an initiation?" I grinned.

Tristan wiggled his eyebrows. "I guess you'll just have to wait and see, won't you?" He then used his hip to nudge me off his chair. "And you have to go. There are eight hours worth of Tweets to read and tumblrs to catch up on. Gossip won't be found on its own. And since you're not giving me the goods, I need to find *someone* who will."

"Seems like Hamlet's Ghost knows a lot. Can you find out who that is?"

"Not yet. Rule number two of journalism: When you reveal a source too early, it's harder to track down secrets. And I'd like some more . . . especially since I'm not getting any from you. And you obviously have some, Ms. I-Went-on-a-Date-with-Eric."

“I didn’t go on a date. We had dinner. But, seriously, if you find out who Hamlet’s Ghost is, can you tell me?”

“We’ll see how useful Hamlet’s Ghost becomes to me. In fact, I’m following him now. Or her.”

“Promise you’ll let me know?” There was a pleading note in my voice that I instantly regretted. It was clear that Tristan wasn’t someone who appreciated showing vulnerability.

“Of course!” Tristan held his pinky high in the air. “Pinky promise.”

I hooked my finger with his, hoping that his version and my version of a promise were the same, but realizing that I honestly had no idea.

CHAPTER 6

Skye Henderon

Good luck with the cast list today, Eric . . . not like you'll need it. Celebratory dinner 2night? #ihearthamlet

Kennedy Clifford

Hope that Zach gets the hint that this semester, I'm keeping the drama onstage only.

Zach Mathis

@alleyesonbree I assume the non-response to my coffee invite means you're not interested. It's cool.

Oops. I read the last Tweet. I'd gotten the invite from the red-haired actor/waiter that O'Dell had kicked out of auditions hours after he'd sent it, when my phone finally turned on, and had completely forgotten about it.

I felt a twinge of guilt. I hadn't meant to ignore him, but that's how it had come across. And while I wouldn't have actually gone out with him — it would have been taken the wrong way by my classmates, especially when they seemed so against friendships with townies — I didn't want him to think I was being mean.

I slid my phone back in my purse and focused on Willow, sitting across the table from me at Hope's Cookies in town.

"What do you think about sheer?" Willow asked. Eric, Chad, and Tad were all playing old-school arcade games in Peace-a-Pizza, the attached pizza parlor next door, and Tristan was still poring over the old records in the thrift store. Usually, the one-mile stretch of Main Street that led from MacHale to the Forsyth Inn could be comfortably seen in an hour, but we'd managed to stretch it into an all-day event. We'd spent an hour at the coffee shop, had poked through the vintage store, and had had an impromptu snowball fight in the town square. We'd talked about the spring social studies trip to Washington, DC; whether Keara Scott had gotten a nose job over break; and whether Ms. Robinette was having an affair with Mr. Bart, the creepy janitor who lived in the Hafner basement. No one had brought up Andi. Or the auditions. And I wasn't sure if it was my imagination or not, but it seemed like Tristan deliberately tried to steer the conversation away from the Hamlet's Ghost account. Whenever I tried to push the conversation in that direction, Tristan would interject by turning the topic toward himself.

"What are we talking about?" As if to prove my point, Tristan drifted toward the tiny café table in the corner Willow and I had commandeered. "Move over." He hip-checked me, forcing me to shift so he could sit on the edge of the seat.

"So, please tell me you're going to make the costumes *sexy* this year. If everyone has to wear, like, shapeless tunics, I'm going to *die*," Tristan said, as if he were simply picking up mid-conversation.

Willow took a small bite of her M&M cookie, then delicately wiped her mouth. "Are you going to write about this?" Willow asked suspiciously.

Tristan shook his head. "Nope. Scout's honor."

"You were never a Scout," Willow scoffed.

"And *you* don't know anything about me. Anyway, spill."

"Well, I guess it depends on who ends up getting cast." Willow turned to me. "How sheer can you go? For costumes, I mean," she clarified. "I saw this cool curtain-like material at the fabric store I'd love to use. I read some feminist analysis of the play, and I feel that could work well. Like, Ophelia is this window into the sickness of society, and she's covered by curtain-like material. Which, eventually, of course, is her own undoing. She can't shake society and society ends up killing her."

"How sheer?" I repeated. I imagined the bright lights hitting the fabric, showing off every single curve. I put the rest of my cookie down. "Not very."

"Why not?" Willow asked.

"Yeah, why not?" Tristan pressed. Even though he didn't have his iPad out on the table, I was sure he was taking mental notes, like everything I said was being committed to his memory. It was both flattering and unsettling.

"Because . . ." I trailed off, once again caught in the push-pull desires of wanting to confide in my new friends and being afraid that they might use whatever I said against me. I didn't want Willow to think I was the lame roomie who lived in the library. I didn't want Tristan to think I was an overeager spotlight-grabber, ready to show off *everything* in front of the MacHale community. "I don't even have the part yet."

"Right, not yet. But I mean, who else would? I heard you were really good."

I felt my stomach unclench a bit. I imagined Eric's hands on my arms, feeling his fingers through the fabric, the audience noticing the chemistry between us just from his grip. "Maybe sheer would be good," I said.

Willow grinned. "Awesome. I think so, too."

"So, what are you thinking for Hamlet?" I asked, trying to imagine Eric onstage in one of Willow's designs.

"What was that look?" Willow laughed. "I think I want to make Hamlet sort of this 1930s player. Think *The Great Gatsby* but with more of an edge. Like, tank tops and suspenders and as few jackets as possible. I want the audience to see his muscles. I mean, because; let's get real, it's Hamlet. Everyone's read it, and no one is that excited to see it. So how do you make it interesting? You've got to make it hot. You've got to make *him* hot." Willow blinked her heavily mascaraed eyes at me as my phone buzzed on the table. I glanced down, relieved that Eric's rice trick had worked, and then felt uneasy when I saw the latest Tweet on my feed.

> **Hamlet's Ghost** @hamletsghost
> Darkness cloaks many of Shakespeare's tragedies, but one thing is crystal clear: the cast of #machalehamlet. Ready to play a part?

"Oh no," I murmured. It was only 1:30, I wasn't ready to see the cast list yet.

"Bree?" Willow asked. Wordlessly, I shoved the phone over to her. "Ugh, I can't believe you're making me look at Twitter!"

Willow sighed good-naturedly, then wrinkled her nose. "Who's Hamlet's Ghost?"

"That's a good question."

"Wait, what did he say?" Tristan asked.

"Don't you know?" I raised my eyebrow at Tristan. I still wasn't entirely sure it *wasn't* him Tweeting.

"Indulge me." He sighed theatrically.

"The cast list is up." The cookie I'd just eaten sat like a rock in my stomach.

"So, that's great news! Do you wanna go now?" Willow asked.

"I guess so." I didn't make any attempt to get out of my seat. Just then, my phone lit up and skittered across the table.

It was a text from Skye.

> Sorry. I thought you were good. And there's always next year. ☺

The smiley face told me everything I needed to know. She'd won.

"I have to go," I choked. I pushed my chair back, allowing the tears to flow as soon as I headed outside. I was both relieved and annoyed Willow hadn't followed me.

I sprinted down Scholar's Walk, not even realizing until my foot landed on the grass that I'd walked the entire path without cutting out early. I barely cared. What worse luck could I have?

The theater lobby was lit and crowded with Forsyth and MacHale students, clambering over one another to peer at the cast list tacked on the bulletin board opposite the Sarah Charonne memorial. I crossed my fingers out of habit and elbowed my way into the crush of students, jockeying for a prime spot to see the list.

Even though, deep down, I knew.

I didn't want to look.

I had to look.

HAMLET CAST LIST

HAMLET	Eric Riley
OPHELIA	Kennedy Clifford
OPHELIA (u/s, matinee)	Skye Henderson
GERTRUDE	Vivy Brownslee
CLAUDIUS	Christian Kent
POLONIUS	Rex Andrews
LAERTES	Kris Owens
ROSENCRANTZ	Chad Connor
GUILDENSTERN	Tad Richman
HORATIO	Brian Vohden
GHOST OF HAMLET'S FATHER	Mr. O'Dell

I ran my finger down the rest of the list as the names and characters swam together. For a second, my brain remained trained on the ghost of Hamlet's father, unable to remove the part from the weird Twitter account.

My name wasn't anywhere. Nowhere. Not even a Third guard or Player number three, which was what Leah Banks had gotten. Even *Leah Banks* had gotten a part. I spotted her in the corner, celebrating with her freshman friends. I turned back to the list. Blinked. Blinked again. Nope. I still wasn't anywhere on the list.

"Sorry, can I see the list?" A blonde girl pushed me aside, not waiting for an answer. I nodded.

She scrunched her face up when she saw my eyes swimming with tears. "Sorry."

"About what?" I snapped. I walked into the theater, relieved that it was dark and quiet and empty. Occasionally, I'd hear a muffled "Yes!" or "Seriously?" echoing from the lobby.

I perched onstage and hugged my knees to my chest. There wouldn't be any late-night rehearsals or sneaking off to split a pizza. No sheer costumes or stolen kisses or calling each other by our characters' names just for fun. No highlighting a script or spending all day pretending to be someone I wasn't. Just weeks of pretending I didn't care about the play. And I wasn't a good enough actress to do that.

I brushed the tears away from my face with the back of my hand. How could I have been such an idiot to believe I had a chance?

"Briana Beland, correct?" a deep voice said behind me.

It was Mr. O'Dell.

"Sorry. I'll leave." I said, hating the tremble in my voice that made it obvious I was crying.

"Hold on a second. Can we talk?"

Could we talk? I could barely even breathe right now. I sat rooted to my spot onstage. Mr. O'Dell stepped forward. "You aren't happy."

I wiped the back of my eyes with my hand and stood up. "I guess I wonder . . . what happened?"

"What happened?" Mr. O'Dell laughed, a short, echoing bark. "Auditions happened. I made my decisions. I posted the cast list. And you're disappointed."

"I was good." My voice was quiet, but definitely audible. I resisted the urge to backtrack, apologize, make it seem like

I didn't mean to say what I said. Because I'd meant to say it. I'd *meant* it.

"You were good," he repeated the sentence back to me.

"So?" My voice echoed in the empty auditorium. The auditorium I *wouldn't* perform in. Another tear leaked out of the corner of my eye and down my cheek. I didn't bother to wipe it away.

"So you know that. And you know sometimes very good actors don't get parts."

I am not looking for a life lesson! I breathed in and out, hating how my tears dripped onto the stage at a furious clip. I'd wanted to work with him. I'd *defended* the whole MacHale-Forsyth alliance. And now, none of it mattered.

"You . . ." I said in a small voice, trying to get the words out. "You called me Ophelia."

"I did?"

I nodded. How did he not remember? I remembered the cold air, the bright light, the way my nerves seemed ready to snap at any second, especially after my run-in with Skye. Hearing *Ophelia* had given me hope that everything would be all right, that I wouldn't be at the center of the rumor mill because people were trying to figure out where I fit in at MacHale. They'd know. I'd be Briana Beland, star of the school play, girlfriend of Eric Riley.

At least Hamlet's Ghost wouldn't be talking about me anymore.

The thought didn't make me feel better.

"I did call you Ophelia." Overdramatic or not, each utterance of the name felt like a knife to my heart. "Sometimes I call actors by the parts I've seen them play in the past. And you were a good Ophelia. But you weren't an honest one."

Tension crackled between us. We were standing facing each other onstage, and I realized that *this* was the type of scene that had energy, that people couldn't help but watch. Deep down, even I wanted to know what would happen and who would make the next move.

"I *am* honest."

"You misunderstood me. I'm not talking about you as a person. I don't even know you. But I do know what I saw onstage, and I know you weren't an honest *Ophelia*. When I saw you onstage, I saw a high school student who had something to prove. Your stakes weren't high enough. Ophelia's stakes are madness or sanity, life or death. Yours were *Am I good enough? How do I prove I'm good enough? Can I show people how much they should like me?* You were interesting to watch, but you weren't Ophelia. And *she* was who I needed to see."

"So now I'm nobody. Thank you," I said stiffly. I'd meant for it to sound angry, but it came out sounding plaintive and sad. And then, to make it even more pathetic, I wiped my face with the back of my sleeve. "I need to go."

"Hold up," Mr. O'Dell said.

I didn't want to turn back around, but I did.

"What?"

"I want you to work on the show. I think it's actually essential you do."

"I don't want to be Andi. I mean . . . I don't want to be the assistant director," I corrected. I wasn't sure why Andi's name had slipped out.

"Andi. Yes. That was unfortunate." Mr. O'Dell shook his head ruefully. "But I don't just need an assistant. I need a creative force who can help me bring this show to the next level. Elevate it, if you will, beyond a simple high school show and into a theatrical performance that won't be easily forgotten. We want to bring in some new dynamics for a new generation. After all, everyone knows *Hamlet.* I want to do something groundbreaking with this production. Something no one's ever done before. And I want you to do it. I know you Tweet, and I think you're funny. I also think you need to do some work on character motivation and separating it from your own. I want to make you the play's social media director."

Social. Media. Director. Of course I'd heard the words before, but I couldn't understand them together. It was made up, some imaginary position to try to make me feel better.

Well, it wouldn't.

And I wouldn't do it.

I shook my head and left the theater. I may not have had a part, but at least I had my dignity.

CHAPTER 7

Leah Banks

@alleyesonaree OMG, Are U OK? LMK if U Want to talk!!

Briana Beland @alleyesonbree

Thanks, but it's all good! Seriously, I'm pretty psyched to have some space in my schedule ☺

Skye Henderson

Can't wait to get my matinee on with Eric. Want to rehearse later tonight?

Skye Henderson

Eric, are you not checking your Twitter feed again? Do I have to call you?

Skye Henderson

Eric?!

I refreshed Skye's Twitter feed, inwardly pleased that Eric seemed to be ignoring her.

Of course, he hadn't exactly been Tweeting a million times per hour at me, but it wasn't like I was reaching out to him. At least I didn't *look* desperate. But I was desperate. I was desperately bored and sadder than I'd ever been first semester. For two glorious days, I'd had a taste of what my MacHale life could have been like. And now, it had been yanked away.

I glanced out the window at the empty campus. While cast members of *Hamlet* were rushing to rehearsal, I had a whole day of nothing yawning in front of me. I just wished the next two weeks would fly by, so second semester would hurry up and start. Once the campus was full of students, I'd be able to slip back into anonymity. Maybe it wouldn't be so bad. I'd already had one semester of empty afternoons and overhearing inside jokes I didn't get. I'd survived. And I'd be able to survive it again.

I picked up the book on my desk. It was *The Magic Mountain*, our required break reading for English. I'd just gotten a few pages in, but I couldn't concentrate. The book was all about a guy who goes to visit his cousin at a sanatorium for tuberculosis patients and ends up getting stuck there for seven years, surrounded by the same people and living the same routine, day in and day out. It was supposed to be an allegory about modern life, or something, and it hit way too close to home right now. I already knew what it was like to feel surrounded and watched, with nowhere to escape. I didn't need to read about it.

Not knowing what else to do, but needing to do something, I spotted a box of hair dye in Willow's dresser. It was a coppery red that I remembered from the beginning of the fall. I grabbed the box and headed into the bathroom.

Twenty minutes later, my hair was orange.

I looked at my reflection with a sense of satisfaction. It wasn't pretty. It was the type of color any disaffected teenager would use, a sign they were done trying to fit in. Because what was the point? Whatever I'd done hadn't been good enough. I couldn't stand out on my talent, and I was sick of trying to blend in.

I left the bathroom and went back to my room. A new Tweet had popped up on my feed.

Tristan Schuler

Get ready for some "drama." Read about it here.

New article!

I clicked on the link and an article from the *MacHale Crier* blog popped up on my screen.

FORSOOTH, FORSYTH!

WHY ADD MORE *DRAMA* TO MACHALE?

We are scholars. We are artists. We are dreamers. We are seekers, here to find the *Maine* difference promised to us by promotional brochures and our illustrious headmistress, Dr. Conger. We are the so-called "Macolytes," the proud upholders of the MacHale tradition who've found this tiny paradise in the woods and made it our own.

And now, it seems, we are an open campus for whoever wants to drop in. The recent decision to open auditions for the Winterm production to students from Forsyth High School was a decision made by Dr. Conger to, in her words, "continue the mutually beneficial relationship between the town of Forsyth and the institution of MacHale." Admirable words and an admirable goal, but why is it that MacHale students are the only ones being asked to sacrifice?

Take, for example, Briana Beland. A transfer to MacHale and loyal member of the drama department, Beland had hopes of nabbing the part of Ophelia in the *Hamlet* production. However, Beland was cruelly overlooked in the audition process and didn't get any part. Now, she's stranded during winter break on the MacHale campus, forced to witness her peers participate in a production without her — all because of the administration's decision to invite the Forsyth community into an already over-enrolled program. They can talk about community and relationship-building all they want, but what do they have to say to Briana Beland, who's been left out in the cold? Forcing us to somehow atone for the subsequent misunderstandings will most likely only serve to further raise the windchill on campus. . . .

I pushed the mouse back, the words swimming in front of me as rage coursed through my veins. Was *that* why Tristan had been so eager to be friendly? Just so he could get some sort of story? And *seriously*? Of course he was Hamlet's Ghost. He used the same flowery, over-the-top language. He stirred up drama. He wasn't my friend.

I'd already lost the part. But Tristan had stolen my dignity.

I grabbed my phone with a clammy hand and texted Tristan.

Come over now.

A tear rolled down my cheek, then another and another. I wiped my eyes and caught sight of myself in the mirror, the coppery-orange dye job clashing with the purple-and-white comforter on my bed.

A few minutes later, there was a knock on my door. "It's open," I called halfheartedly, not bothering to wipe away my tears.

Tristan walked in, his mouth dropping in horror. "What did you do to yourself? Bree, honey, is this a cry for help?"

"Hello, Tristan," I said flatly.

"Looks like someone dyed," he said. "Ha! Lame joke."

"It was a lame joke. And an even *lamer* article. Why did you *do* that?" I exploded. "Weren't you supposed to write about the dangers of battery-eating or something?"

"I did write the battery piece. I just didn't Tweet it. I thought this topic was more interesting. And also, FYI, I wrote it for *you*."

"You made me look like a *loser*."

A shocked expression crossed Tristan's face. "Loser? No. I made you look like a heroine. I'm giving you a spotlight, babe. I thought you'd like it."

"I don't." I shook my head.

Tristan enveloped me into a hug. Despite myself, I leaned in as a fresh sob rose to my throat.

Tristan pulled away. "Did you just blow your nose on my shirt?"

"No! Though you'd deserve it."

"You better not have. Because I can deal with emotions. I can't deal with *fluids*."

"Sorry," I said sulkily. He seemed utterly unphased by my reaction.

"It's okay. I guess we're even. And I know, I know, I should have asked you. But I didn't have time. And it'll get you the attention you deserve. For the *right* reasons, not the hair situation. Which you need to explain."

My hands flew up to cover my head, as if that would do anything. "I needed a change," I said coolly.

"You needed a friend," Tristan said. "That is *not* your color."

"Well, since I'm not in the play, it doesn't really matter, does it?"

"It does matter, because that hair color makes it clear that you're having a breakdown. It's an expression of hostility."

"I'm not hostile toward anyone!" I said, knowing my tone made it clear that wasn't the case. "I mean, Mr. O'Dell told me why I didn't get the part. He said I wasn't 'honest enough.' And whatever, he's the one who has the final say."

"Yeah, but maybe he would have thought differently if the Forsyth kids hadn't been there," Tristan said. "Have you thought about that? All of a sudden, it's double the competition."

"Of course the idea crossed my mind," I said casually. As if the images weren't constantly swarming in my head: Groups of kids running to Peace-a-Pizza or Hope's Cookies during a quick rehearsal break to grab snacks. Inside jokes shared in the green room. Eric and Kennedy making eyes at each other from across the stage. Eric and Skye running lines in her room . Skye always giving me that incredibly insincere *It's so sad* puppy-dog expression. It was like a bad movie I couldn't turn off. "But thinking about it doesn't change anything."

"So you agree with my article. You would have gotten a part if the Forsyth kids weren't there, and they took your opportunity. Isn't that right?" Tristan asked.

"I don't *know*!" I exploded. "I mean, Kennedy was good. And at the end of the day, if Kennedy hadn't been there, the part would have gone to Skye. Thanks for trying to help, but you didn't. And next time you write about me, ask first, okay? Or just stick to the dead students who can't speak for themselves."

I turned to go, but Tristan pulled me back. "So, what are you going to do? After you dye your hair back from *pumpkin*. You still haven't told me why you decided to do that."

"I needed a change. The box said red. Not everything has to have a *story*."

"But your hair is now *orange*," Tristan countered. "Seriously, *you*, Bree, darling, are turning into a tragic heroine, whether you know it or not."

"I'm not *tragic*. If you want tragedy, write about Andi."

"Andi isn't tragic. Andi is dumb. And she has nothing to do with the real story, which is that MacHale still feels guilty over the Sarah Charonne murder. You know that Andi won't be remembered in twenty years, but if Sarah hadn't been murdered twenty years ago, then Forsyth would never be involved in the play, and you'd be Ophelia, don't you?"

"I don't think some dead girl from twenty years ago has any control over my life," I said sharply. "And stop turning *my life* into *your story*."

My phone buzzed, breaking the silence. It was my mother. *Ugh.* That would be the worst part of the entire ordeal. To tell my mom, after everything, my best wasn't good enough. And she'd be sympathetic, which would make it even worse. With my luck, she'd probably *cry* on the phone. I let the call go to voice mail. "I think I just need to be by myself for a bit. I'm not good company right now," I said.

"But *I'm* stellar company," Tristan said. "You shouldn't have to deal with this alone. And I still need to get you to forgive me. I know you're still mad."

I gave him a hard look. "But since you offered, you can begin by making it up to me with a Hope's Cookies brownie. And *not* a half-price one you got because it was after six p.m. A full-priced one *only*. And that's just to start."

But Tristan wasn't listening. Instead, he was squinting down at his iPhone screen.

"Did you even hear what I said?" I asked, sighing as I felt my anger ebbing and the sadness creeping back in. It didn't matter whether or not Tristan wrote an article; the reality was still the same. I didn't have a part. I wasn't part of the play. And I had to do *something*. It was a MacHale requirement that any student on campus for Winterm had to participate in an activity. I could play a sport or build houses for Habitat for Humanity or spend weekends making trails at the state park. I could try out for the science bowl. I could work for the newspaper and have Tristan as my editor. Nothing sounded appealing.

I thought again about Mr. O'Dell's offer. *Social media director?* On the surface, it sounded like torture. Every single day, I would have to face the fact that I hadn't gotten cast. I'd have to watch Skye act, both onstage and in her sympathetic glances toward me. Once again, I'd be relegated to the background as Briana. But it was the only way I could stay involved. I could still see Eric. I could still be a part of the energy backstage. If I loved theater, I would do it.

I stood up and yanked my hair back into a ponytail. "I need to go. I'll see you later." I stood up and walked out of the room, leaving Tristan behind as I headed to the theater.

"Please let it be empty," I whispered as I pushed open the door.

It wasn't. Students were clumped in groups, gossiping, chatting, and laughing. And maybe it was my imagination, but I thought I heard someone suck in their breath before lowering their voice to a whisper as I walked by.

There goes the loser who didn't get a part.

Of course, I couldn't hear the exact words anyone was saying, but what else could it have been? Which only made it more urgent that I prove that I wasn't the sad, lonely, *tragic* person Tristan pegged me as in the newspaper story. I hurried backstage, relieved at the quiet surrounding me.

While the auditorium itself was both cozy and majestic, with its skylight, rough-hewn benches, and dark wooden stage, the backstage area was barnlike and cramped. A balcony-like loft accessible by a narrow wooden staircase ringed the space, joining the metallic catwalk that led to the lights crossing the auditorium ceiling. Metal cages filled with costumes, props, and stage crew supplies dotted the loft, giving off the appearance of a prison. At one end of the loft was an unmarked metal door that led to the windowless drama office. At the other was a gate that separated the loft from the catwalk, barred with a metal chain and a Do Not Enter sign.

I picked my way through the maze of mismatched tables and chairs, clothing racks, and varying sizes of plywood beams covering the floor. As I headed to the staircase that led to the drama office, someone stepped out from the shadows and blocked my path.

It was Skye, eyeing me with the same look of suspended disdain that Dr. Conger gave any student who slunk late into chapel. It was a look that said *We both know you messed up, but I'm going to do you a favor and not embarrass you further by saying anything.* It was a look far worse than simply being called out, because it made you feel like an idiot for the entire day.

"Why are you here?" she asked. "Mr. O'Dell is *very strict* about having closed rehearsals. That means cast only. Sorry." She gave me an *I'm not sorry at all* smile.

"I didn't know you were the assistant director," I said icily.

"I'm *not*. I'm *Ophelia*." Her slate-gray eyes narrowed, as if willing me to correct her and say that, actually, she was only the understudy. I wouldn't give her that satisfaction.

"And *I* have a meeting with Mr. O'Dell." Not waiting for a response, I sidestepped her and hurried up the rickety steps into the tiny theater office.

At the door, I could hear strains of weird chanting music emanating from the room, far different than the Broadway-musical cast recordings Dr. Spidell used to play. I raised my hand to knock, but before I could, the door swung open.

"Ms. Beland, it's good to see you again. Come in." He opened the door farther and gestured inside. I glanced around at the bare floors and stark walls. When it was Dr. Spidell's office, the floor had been covered with old VHS tapes of past performances, and every square inch of wall had been covered with brightly colored posters from musicals.

"Sit." He gestured to the top of a rickety filing cabinet as he took a seat in the director's chair next to his desk. BRECKIN was embroidered in thick white script. *What type of name is Breckin, anyway?* I thought savagely. Mr. O'Dell must have caught my expression, because his own soured, too, from one of bemused indifference to one of vague hostility. But then I smiled, and it was gone, as though I'd imagined it.

"I read the article about the cast list. I'm sorry to have heard how upset you were. And I only wish you and I could have properly talked before you aired your grievances to the public at large. Because I think we had a misunderstanding. And here's the thing I didn't get a chance to tell you before." He rested his chin on his steepled fingers. "You *are* good. I wasn't just saying that to make you feel better about yourself. I don't do that. When I saw you onstage, my first thought was that you were good. You've got presence, your voice carries, and I want to know more about you. But . . ."

Here it came: But I wasn't good *enough.* That I should really pay more attention in bio and consider going on the pre-med track once I got to college. I braced myself, hoping that at *least* whatever acting skills I had would be enough to not cause me to cry until after I left the office.

"I don't think you understand *acting*. That was what I'd been trying to tell you yesterday, but I think I lost you when I said it wasn't an honest performance. And that wasn't the right word. It was an honest performance. But it wasn't Ophelia's performance. You were doing it for you. You cried real tears. I saw that. But they weren't Ophelia's tears. They were the tears of a girl who desperately wants validation. And that's not what I need. And it's not what you need, either. Trust me, I've seen actresses like you before, the ones who crave the spotlight. They aren't being true to the *art*. The world needs more *artists*. Not more performers. And this *Hamlet* is going to be a work of art. I'm very excited. And I would like you to play a part in my vision. What do you think?"

I narrowed my eyes, not sure which part of his speech was most insulting. While I pondered, Mr. O'Dell stood up and began pacing the room, as though he was performing a monologue.

"The theater is all about *trust*. You have to trust in yourself to create a believable character the audience will root for. And I saw someone onstage who is very good . . . no, more than good — who is *gifted* when it comes to adopting different roles. But none of the roles were anchored. Does that make sense?"

I nodded, which only made the tears welling at the corners of my eyes trickle down my face.

"I know you're not listening. And that's all right," he said gently. "What's important is that you came back to *Hamlet*. And I promise that this performance, and your part in it, will go down in history. We're revolutionizing the genre. Trust me."

I nodded, not making eye contact. If he thought I was so great, then why didn't he give me a chance? How *revolutionary* could Tweeting about the show be? I wiped my eyes with the back of my sleeve. I had nothing left to lose, just one more chance to make Mr. O'Dell reconsider his decision.

"I just . . . Theater is really important to me. And I . . ." I choked back a sob, because I couldn't tell him the truth: that theater was everything. That I belted out Broadway show tunes whenever I was in the shower. That I turned my Spotify playlist to private just so no one would know how many times I'd listened to the *Smash* soundtrack. That I'd read *Moon for the*

Misbegotten so many times I had it memorized. That theater was a chance for me to not be quiet, to not be average, to not be *me*. That I "tried really hard." I shrugged, shook my head, and mustered a smile. "But I'll be okay."

Mr. O'Dell nodded. "You see, *that* is what I needed to see onstage. Your truth, as manifested by Ophelia. Here, I see vulnerability and sadness and confusion. Onstage, I saw competition. I'm not saying you're not good, because I can tell that you have potential. And I want to bring it out if you'll let me. This will be good for you as an actress. Don't think of the social media director gig as some assignment to keep you busy. Think of it as playing Hamlet on Twitter!"

"So you want me to Tweet quotes and stuff?"

Mr. O'Dell shook his head. "I most adamantly do *not* want you to Tweet quotes and stuff. What I want is for you to really find the voice of the play and Tweet it to everyone. What's the behind-the-scenes gossip? What's the drama? What would Hamlet think of it? I want everything from asking people if Hamlet would rather watch baby panda videos or baby hippo videos on YouTube, to getting input on design choices. We want this *Hamlet* to be interactive, and you will be the one to help us break the fourth wall and make the audience essential to our theatrical journey."

"I . . . see," I said, even though I didn't, not at all. This was even worse than being an understudy. That was the same as a kindergartener being told she was important because she got to help pick up the blocks after playtime. This was Mr. O'Dell thinking that I would actually be *happy* to do something like this, like he was doing me a favor. And the worst was that *I was going to do it.*

"I don't Tweet," Mr. O'Dell said, lost in thought. "I don't like it. I think it's for cowards. Anything worth saying needs to be said, not typed. But I also know that we're in the spotlight with this play, full pun intended. I wasn't pleased to have read that sophomoric Op-Ed in the student newspaper by someone who clearly doesn't know anything about art. And as much as I loathe to admit it, we need to have a counterattack ready. And they will not batter our fourth wall with their iPhones and Facebooks and Instagrams. We will break it ourselves, one Tweet at a time. It's revolutionary, in a way!" He turned back to his computer. It was clear I was dismissed.

"So . . ." I had a million questions. *What does that mean? When do I start? Do I have to do it?*

"Congratulations, Ms. Beland. You are the official social media director of *Hamlet*. Now get thee to a laptop!"

I hurried down the stairs, wanting to be able to get out of the auditorium as quickly as possible while seeing as few people as possible.

No such luck.

Skye stood sentry at the bottom of the stairs. I tried to brush past her, but she grabbed on to my elbow.

"What happened?" she asked, her eyes wide. "Did he yell at you? He yells a lot."

"No. I'm the social media director of the play. It's awesome!" The words tumbled out before I had time to consider my strategy.

Skye scrunched her nose. "What does that mean?"

"You'll see. But Mr. O'Dell is very excited. We both think it's going to make the play awesome." I forced myself to smile, even though I was lying through my teeth. I saw a shadow of doubt cross Skye's face, and that was all I needed. It wasn't like she was jealous, but I had put her a little bit on edge. This could be fun.

And as I walked out of the auditorium, something even more awesome occurred to me: I'd just been given orders to keep a close eye on Eric. Maybe there *were* worse ways to spend Winterm.

CHAPTER 8

Tristan Schuler

Calling @alleyesonbree to her room for an #itcouldbeworse gossip session. Crying encouraged, carbs included.

I saw the Tweet too late. My key was in the lock as I refreshed my phone. And before I could turn around and sneak away, Willow opened the door, escorting me into our bedroom.

Tristan sat on my bed. Chad was on the floor. Tad was lounging on Willow's bed. "Pizza?" Tristan held up his half-eaten slice.

"Oh . . . I was going to . . . go to the gym. I was supposed to meet with Laura," I lied.

"I saw Laura head out for a run half an hour ago. I guess you missed her," Willow said.

"Too bad," I said, my stomach sinking as I ran out of excuses.

"You don't want to *run*, you want to eat carbs, right?" Tristan asked.

I ignored him. I didn't want to speak to him. The earlier peace we'd forged was tentative, and I was too exhausted to plaster a fake smile on my face and pretend everything was fine around Tristan. It was *too much* acting.

"It's tragic," Tristan said dramatically as he grabbed a slice of pizza. He delicately pulled off the pepperoni slices, then blotted the grease with a napkin.

"What's tragic? That you're going to waste perfectly good pizza? Or that this pizza tastes like something you'd find in Tad's sock pile? Why do we always order from Peace-a-Pizza?" Willow asked as she reached over and snatched the abandoned pepperoni from his plate.

"What's *tragic* is that Tristan uses that word too much. *Seriously*," I said crisply, finally succumbing to a slice. Tristan was right. The cheese was soggy and tasteless.

"Me-*ow*!" Tad said. "I didn't know Bree had a mean-girl side."

"Kidding!" I said brightly.

"No, I think it's good. You should be *meaner* to Tristan. He's always mean to me. Not to mention how badly he treats my sock pile, which I think might actually be coming to life. It moves on its own," Tad said in an exaggerated whisper.

"I seriously *have* to get a single, stat. Not only for my mental health, but clearly, my safety is also being compromised by living with you," Tristan whined. "But I don't have time to focus on myself right now. I am turning my attention to Bree's unfortunate medical issue."

"What are you talking about?" I asked, the bite of pizza I'd just swallowed lodging in my throat and causing me to cough.

Tristan took in my over-the-top reaction and laughed. "Someone's hiding something. Seriously, you got so suspicious! And I'm talking about your *obvious* lack of backbone. Unless you also have a secret cell-phone-eating habit."

"Ugh, it's too soon." Willow grimaced. "And Bree has a backbone."

"Recent behavior suggests otherwise. Why are you even working on the play? I thought you decided not to do it?"

I arched an eyebrow. Clearly, Tristan had sources everywhere. My social media director position hadn't even been officially announced.

"Well, I needed to do *some* extracurricular. And I like theater. Besides, what good does not doing the play do? O'Dell won't care. It'll just make me miserable. And O'Dell wanted me to be the social media director. If I *hadn't* said yes, I'd never get cast in anything ever again."

"I disagree. And just giving in like that is making *me* miserable." Tristan sighed.

I shot him a look.

"Well, that's *your* problem. And I don't think it's giving in. It's actually cool. I'm working with the design team and the production team to give a behind-the-scenes look into the play. But, like, in the voice of Hamlet. It's creative. It'll be fun." I was lying through my teeth and I knew it, I just hoped Tristan didn't. "I can write about costumes and stuff, so think about what you want me to say."

"I have some initial costume ideas if you want to Tweet the pictures." Willow hopped up and flipped through the sketchbook on her desk. "But this is *not* me approving of Twitter."

I managed to force a smile. "Can we just not talk about the play anymore?" I pulled my laptop from my desk and to my knees.

"Look, I got five more followers," I said to no one in particular. I recognized some of the avatars — Kennedy, Tad, the large guy named Rex from Forsyth who'd been cast as Polonius, and two other names I didn't recognize.

"And I think that you can give up the ghost, Tristan. Give me the password. And then you're off the hook for the cookies."

"Bree, seriously? For the millionth time, I'm not the ghost. I'm actually offended that you think I was. What it Tweets is so *boring*."

"Fine." I didn't want to drop the subject. Tristan was the ghost. He *had* to be.

As I tried to think of ways to get him to admit it, the door swung open and I found myself staring at Eric's shorts-clad legs. I glanced up as Eric smiled sympathetically and held out a bag of gummy bears toward me.

"Thought you could use these," he said, stepping into the room.

"Thanks." I didn't reach over to take the bag. Seeing him, holding the bag of plastic candy out as a consolation prize, only reminded me that he hadn't been there for me right after the cast list came out. That was when I needed someone. Not now. "Congratulations on your part. It's great. *Really*."

"Thanks." Eric grabbed a slice of pizza, then sat down on the floor. He opened the bag of candy and sprinkled the bears on top of the cheese as if he were doing something as normal as sprinkling garlic powder onto a slice.

Tristan lunged for my laptop.

"What are you doing?" I asked.

"This is newsworthy!" He handed my laptop back to me.

Briana Beland @alleyesonbree
Seems the #machalehamlet may owe his cast list success to one sweet secret. Wouldn't you like to know what it is?

"See?" Tristan raised an eyebrow. "That's what people want to hear."

"That is pretty good," I admitted. "Hamlet's Ghost couldn't have done better," I pushed.

"For the millionth time, I'm *not* Hamlet's Ghost." Tristan shook his head. "But if you want me to take over *your* account, let me know. I could gossip about people all day."

"What are you saying about me?" Eric asked, his mouth full.

"I'm turning you into an Internet sensation, one Tweet at a time. And Bree's enabling me."

Eric shrugged. "Whatever." He turned to me. "I'm sorry about the cast list. I wanted to talk to you earlier, especially after I read the article, but things just got . . ." He trailed off. "You know how it is."

I nodded, even though I didn't know how it was, not at all. I wasn't the star of the school play. He was. I imagined his cell exploding with congratulatory texts. I imagined Skye calling him to rehearse. I imagined the Forsyth girl who'd gotten the part of Ophelia shyly introducing herself to him. It was too much.

"It's fine. It's just one play," I said stiffly.

Eric nodded, clearly unconvinced. "You'll get it next time."

"Right."

I sighed and Tristan smirked. I knew he was about to say something about how bad a job I was doing of hiding my disappointment, and I didn't want to hear it.

"Anyway, look on the bright side, Bree. You have two weeks of freedom. You can do whatever; Ms. Robinette is barely around. Just think of it like vacation," Willow said. "I mean, I'm around. I'm only doing costume stuff some of the time, and the rest of the time we can hang out. It'll be fun, I promise."

"And speaking of *fun*, what are we doing tonight?" Tristan asked expectantly.

"There's a party in town. Better than hanging out on campus," Eric suggested.

My stomach fell. This was the looped scene in my mind come to life: Eric and the rest of the cast were beginning to bond and leave me behind. I'd known it was going to happen. I just hadn't expected it to happen so quickly. It had taken me a whole semester to actually get the courage to interact with MacHale kids outside of class. And the Forsyth kids were doing it within hours. Just another way they were clearly more talented than I was.

"A townie party?" Tristan shook his blue-streaked head. "No."

Eric raised an eyebrow in annoyance. "Seriously, dude?"

I felt a flash of jealousy. Why was Eric bonding with Forsyth kids? Of course, that was something I *liked* about Eric in the first place, the fact that he didn't seem to care about the division between the school and the town. But part of me felt miffed he didn't see Tristan's side of the story: That having Forsyth involved in the play had ruined *my* chances of being in the show.

"Yes, *seriously*," Tristan said. "I chose to go to MacHale. I didn't choose to live in *Forsyth*. And the idea of wandering through the woods in freezing-cold weather to hang out in some rec room sounds depressing."

"So you just want to hang out in the dorm all day? All right, bro. Rock out." Eric shrugged and rose to his feet. "Anyone else coming?"

Chad and Tad shook their heads. Willow shrugged. And I realized: This was my chance to be alone with Eric.

"I think it sounds fun," I said boldly. I jumped to my feet.

"Awesome. Willow?" Eric asked.

Willow draped her arm over Tad's shoulders. "Nah. We're going to be boring." Tad's face lit up at the attention.

"Bree, I *command* you not to go. It will *not* be fun," Tristan said sternly. "Who *knows* what goes on at townie parties? It's like you're heading out into the wilderness. You can't even get good cell reception in Forsyth. Has anyone else noticed that?" He looked around.

Eric shook his head. "Anywhere more than five feet away from your laptop is outside your comfort zone," he said before turning to me. "Bree, you ready?"

I looked down. I was wearing a pair of leggings and an ancient gray oversize MacHale sweatshirt that used to be my mother's. Not exactly a party-worthy outfit, but at this point, I stood to gain more by pretending to be confident, carefree Bree than insecure Briana.

I nodded. "All set."

"Bye, guys!" Tad said readily, clearly excited to have Willow to himself, once he got rid of Chad. Tristan stood up and slung his messenger bag over his shoulder.

"Well, I guess I'll just go and make my own fun," he said to no one in particular as he skulked out of the room.

"His badditude is out of control this year, don't you think?" Willow asked once the door had closed behind him. "I swear he didn't used to be such a snob."

"Have you seen his coffee collection?" Tad asked. "Snob city."

Eric shrugged. "Tristan will always be Tristan. He loves the spotlight. He just wants attention."

"Right, and then he'll complain about the temperature of the fountains, or the lack of hot yoga classes during gym." Willow rolled her eyes. "I mean, whatever, Tristan is harmless, but why does he have to be so negative?"

Eric shrugged. "He can be miserable, for all I care. I'm doing drama, I don't need a daily dose in my real life. Ready, Bree?" he asked again, making it clear the conversation was over. I quickly pulled on my parka and yanked a hat down over my still-orangish hair.

The temperature had dropped into the teens since the sun went down, and the wind stung my face. I had a momentary urge to turn around and head back into the warmth of our room. I didn't want to explain to the other party attendees who I was, then follow it with an explanation of how psyched I was to be the social media director of the play. For that matter, I didn't want to explain what the social media director position was in the first place. I wished Eric and I could just skip the party and hang out alone together.

"I really liked that restaurant we went to the other day. I keep thinking about it. The dining hall food has *sucked* this week. I had a jelly sandwich for dinner. They didn't even have peanut butter," I said, hoping he'd get the hint and suggest we grab something to eat in town.

"So is that why you're shivering? Because you don't have enough nutrients?"

"Ha-ha, no." I tried to rein in my disappointment. "So, who's having this party?"

"Kennedy. She lives right across the tracks, over on Duffy."

"Cool." My teeth chattered. I wished more than anything I

could slip my hand in Eric's. A few days ago, I'd been delusional enough to imagine that possibility. Eric himself had said he didn't care if people were gossiping that we were a couple. But now, though he was friendly as ever, he was friendly in the way an RA or an admissions ambassador would be. There were no more knowing glances, or sly grins. Clearly, he liked his girlfriends to have star potential.

"So, are you excited?" I asked as we reached the edge of the woods.

"Yeah, I am." Eric nodded. "I know I was kind of down on Hamlet, but that's because I was sick of the whole ye olde Shakespeare thing. I love that O'Dell wants to make it a little more contemporary. Hamlet as a high school student, Hamlet's father as some corporate CEO who makes bad business decisions . . ." He trailed off. "Look, I know you don't think the social media director gig is that awesome. But I think it's just because you haven't heard his vision. He really wants Twitter to be an integral part. It's like you're the voice of the play. There's a ton of opportunity there."

"You don't need to say that." His false enthusiasm was enough to make me cringe.

"I'm not just saying it. O'Dell chose you to be the one to bring it to life. Meanwhile, I'll be the one getting yelled at by O'Dell for forgetting all my lines," Eric said ruefully.

"You'll be amazing. Seriously, I can't wait to see it."

"Well, I can't wait to see what you do with the social media. O'Dell was talking all about how the play is still really contemporary because of all the lies and secrets and misunderstandings. . . . Like, he loves the idea of all the characters holding iPhones and iPads onstage. He wants us to imagine there's this whole network of secrets that's occurring simultaneously with the action."

"Sounds like MacHale, doesn't it?" I asked. We'd reached the split-rail fence that separated the cemetery from the rest of the property.

"Secrets?" Eric shook his head. "No way. Everyone knows everything that's going on at MacHale. Sometimes even before it happens."

"I feel like I'm out of the loop, then."

Eric shook his head. "Not true. If you weren't in it before, you're in it now."

"Is that a good thing?" I asked with a smile, hoping to lure some of our previous banter back into the conversation.

"That depends." Eric shrugged. "Once you're in The Bubble . . ." Eric trailed off as I swung one leg over the fence. Before I realized it, my foot was firmly planted on one of the flat grave markers.

"I'm surprised you did that," Eric said, sliding onto the ground behind me.

"Did what?" I asked.

"Stepped on the grave. I thought you were Ms. Superstition."

"That stopped about the same time I realized splinters aren't good luck. Look, I still have a scar." I held my index finger in Eric's sightline.

If this were a play, he'd reach out, pull it to his lips, and kiss it to make it better. My mind drifted to the musical *The Fantasticks*. It was one of my favorites, about young love, and about how sometimes, adversity only makes you stronger as a couple. It was sweet and simple script, exactly the type of script I wished I had for . . . whatever Eric and I were doing.

But he didn't. He simply winced sympathetically. I glanced at the marker below my feet, then leaned down to wipe the snow off it.

EMILY MASTERS, 1792–1823

"I'm sure Emily wouldn't mind, right?" I asked.

"Let's hope," Eric said dubiously.

"Eric! *You're* not supposed to be superstitious!" My heart hammered against my chest like an anvil. I felt like *something* was about to happen. I just wasn't sure if it was something good or something bad. I crossed my fingers, hoping for good.

Eric dusted off the gravestone looming in front of him. While most of the grave markers were rectangular stones that lay flat on the ground, this was a proper tombstone. A gargoyle-like statue of an angel flanked it. He leaned in to read the lettering.

"Woah," he breathed out.

"What?"

"Breckin O'Dell."

A shiver launched up my spine. "What?" I squeezed in next to him. The lettering was faint and faded, and the old-fashioned, elaborate script made the individual letters hard to read. I traced them with my fingers.

I whirled around, expecting to see someone in the darkness. Nothing. In the distance, an owl hooted. A tree branch cracked. My heart hammered wildly against my chest. *Nothing.*

"I guess it's a common name." Eric shrugged.

I couldn't tear my eyes away from the headstone. The date read 1822. Eric was right. It was just a coincidence. Even though Breckin didn't sound like a very old fashioned name.

"Officially freaked out. Let's go."

"Sorry. I didn't mean to scare you. I feel like it happens a lot when we're together."

"Better than being scared by myself."

"You have a point." I felt the warmth emanating from Eric's body as we stood up and made our way through the woods. I concentrated on the sounds of our footsteps crunching in the snow and the foggy puffs of air visible in the moonlight.

"I'm just really on edge. But I'm fine," I added quickly.

We'd reached the edge of the woods, and I was able to shake off some of the weirdness. It was strange, but it was a coincidence.

"You say that a lot, you know," Eric said. "'I'm *fine*.' *Fine*. For a girl who has pretty much every single Shakespeare play memorized, that's such a boring word!"

"So I can't even *complain* well enough. That's great." I'd meant for it to be a joke, but the words came out short and angry. I continued to walk, not looking at Eric. I jammed my hands in my pocket, marching forward even though I had no idea where we were going.

"Bree," Eric said softly.

"What?"

"You don't need to be fine. That's all I meant. We're audition buddies, now and forever. And you know what that means?" he asked softly.

I didn't bother to stop walking. He was now several feet behind me, and I raised my voice for him to hear me over the howling January wind. "That that's probably the last time we'll see each other, since you'll be at rehearsal all the time?" My voice sounded snarky and sharp. "Kidding," I added lamely.

Eric caught up to me and I stood silently. My tears had stopped, but I knew if I turned toward him, I would begin crying all over again.

"Look, it sucks to not get a part in the show. I know it. If you'd seen me freshman year . . ." He stopped. "I know what it's like. And I make time for what's important. Always," Eric said. "We don't have to pretend with each other. We do that for the rest of the world. But we're connected now."

"He even gave himself a part," I said in a small voice.

"I know. That was weird. But I guess he wants the ghost of Hamlet's father to be, like, older. Like a dad figure. He's not doing it from onstage, it'll just be his voice booming from the catwalk."

"Still," I sniffled.

"Still, he's just being a weird director. But that's just one person. It doesn't mean you're not a good actress."

"I bet you've never been rejected from anything," I said.

Eric laughed, a short bark that mirrored my own sharp tone. "That's a fantasy."

"What happened?" I asked. Just then, a gust of wind rose up, causing snow from the tree branches above to dump down on our heads.

Eric laughed and brushed the powder from his head and shoulders.

"That's a sign we've got to get out of the cold. All right, Tropical Plant, let's go."

"Tropical Plant?" I asked.

Eric smiled. "Yeah. Because you're so sensitive. To temperatures, I mean."

"Not just temperatures," I said quietly, but Eric didn't hear me above the wind. I quickened my pace to keep up with him.

Duffy Street was a small cul-de-sac located west of the railroad tracks, dotted with more abandoned lots than one-level houses. Eric pulled out his phone, frowning at the display.

"Look for 118," he directed.

I glanced at the house closest to me. 112. "It should be a few up," I said.

We stepped onto the cracked sidewalk and slowly walked past an abandoned lot, then came to a small house set back from the road. The house was painted red and looked like a child's approximation of a gingerbread house, with a falling-apart roof and one shutter lopsidedly hanging from a single hinge.

"I guess this is it," Eric said dubiously.

"We could always go someplace else," I said, still holding out hope he'd ask me if I was down with skipping the party and heading to the Trusty Ax to grab a pizza. I wanted to be alone with Eric. I didn't have to act effortlessly cool like I did with Willow, or super snarky the way I was with Tristan. I could be myself.

"It looks kind of quiet," Eric said dubiously.

That was an understatement. There only seemed to be one light on in the house, barely visible from the window. It didn't look like this was the location of a happening party. It didn't even seem possible that a happening party could fit in the space.

Eric nodded uncertainly, clearly torn. "I said I'd come. I should at least *try*." He bounded to the door and rang the bell while I hung back.

Almost instantly, the door swung open, held by the *real* Ophelia, aka Kennedy Clifford. She was wearing a pair of gray sweatpants and a black camisole, and it looked as though she was in her pajamas, except for the fact her hair hung in loose curls around her shoulders and her green eyes were carefully lined with thick black eyeliner. Her face fell as her gaze moved beyond Eric's shoulder and landed on me.

"Oh," Kennedy said flatly, then turned on an insta-big, insta-fake smile. "You brought someone!"

"Yeah, this is Bree. She's also doing the play."

My shoulders tightened. Skye already had me on edge. I never imagined there would be *another* girl vying for Eric's attention.

"Right. Who are you playing again?" The frostiness in Kennedy's voice made it very clear that she'd scrutinized the cast list and knew I wasn't officially any character.

"I'm the social media director." My teeth chattered. I was *freezing*. Was she going to invite us in or not? Or would she invite *Eric* in, leaving me out in the cold — literally. And if she *did* only invite Eric in, would he accept, or would he leave in solidarity? And if we *did* leave, would we go to the Trusty Ax and sit in a corner booth, and then would he turn toward me and allow his lips to graze mine. . . .

"Got it." Kennedy's sharp tone broke my reverie. "I wasn't expecting you. But that's cool. I mean, if you're cool watching the movie version of *Hamlet*. It might be boring for you. Given that you don't *really* have a part."

"I won't be bored," I said coolly.

"Is anyone else here?" Eric finally asked, glancing over Kennedy's shoulder into the silent house.

"No, no one else showed up. So I guess it's just the three of us!"

"What a surprise." I said icily.

"Well, you know what they say. Two's company. And three's even more merrier. So come on in!" Kennedy stepped aside from the door to let us through.

"Yup, that's exactly what they say. Actually, it's not. You know that, right?" I asked.

Kennedy shook her head. "Nope. I go to public school, remember?" she asked sweetly.

Eric glanced between us.

"I don't care where you go to school," I said, forcing a smile.

"I didn't mean to crash," Eric said awkwardly. "But I think you guys might have a lot in common. Kennedy loves Shakespeare, too!"

That's not the only thing she loves, I thought, annoyed at Eric's oblivion.

And then I realized he probably didn't know what was going on. Just like he didn't believe in superstition, it was also clear that subtext wasn't one of his specialties. He was used to being admired and adored. To borrow Kennedy's butchering of the phrase, he was the epitome of *the more, the merrier*.

"Well, come in," Kennedy said as we trailed behind her, across the threshold into the house. It was even smaller on the inside than it looked on the outside, and almost every single surface was covered with piles of paper. Something brushed against my leg and I screamed.

Eric and Kennedy looked at me, startled.

"Oh, that's just Brutus." Kennedy reached down and picked up a large orange cat. She hissed loudly. "She didn't mean to scare you, did she?" Kennedy whispered in Brutus's ear. Eric chuckled.

"Bree's afraid of everything," he announced.

Kennedy put Brutus down and shrugged.

"No. I'm not. Scared of anything." I gave them both a tight-lipped smile. While she may have gotten the part, she wasn't going to get Eric. At least not without a fight. "So, which one are we watching? The Kenneth Branagh one?" I asked pointedly, proving that I wasn't about to take the bait.

"Oh, yeah," Kennedy said. "Here, let's go down to the basement." She opened a plain wooden door that led to a narrow flight of stairs.

"Hold on, let me get the light." She headed down into the darkness. Seconds later, a bare bulb above us lit up, casting a dim light on the concrete walls below us. A leather love seat sat on a threadbare rug facing a television. "I'm sure this doesn't look anything like the *palace-like dorms* you guys live in, but it serves its purpose."

I softened a tiny bit. "This is what my rec room back home looks like," I offered, trying to let her know that it wasn't her *house* that unleashed my bitter side. "If we'd have known it was a movie-watching party, we'd have brought popcorn."

"Yup," Eric agreed, and I felt a momentary thrill that, for a brief moment, he saw us as a *we*.

"Oh, there's some upstairs. Can you make it, Bree? I need to make sure the movie has finished downloading. It keeps stopping on my laptop." Kennedy frowned.

I glanced at Eric, hoping he'd suggest we make the popcorn together. But he'd already plopped on the couch.

"Okay . . ." I agreed dubiously, wanting to make it perfectly clear to Kennedy that I knew exactly what she was doing. "Good luck with getting the movie to work."

"Popcorn is in the cupboard, microwave's on the counter. Thank you!"

Careful not to trip over Kennedy's psycho cat, I made my way to the kitchen and put the popcorn in the microwave, trying to ignore the sound of Kennedy's and Eric's laughter wafting up from the floorboards in between pops. I glanced at the refrigerator, covered in a Kennedy-focused collage. There were pictures of Kennedy as a kid at a dance recital, her gap-toothed smile eagerly turning toward the camera. Kennedy in pigtails and a cowboy hat, at some sort of talent competition, braces on her teeth and a preteen pout evident on her face. So she'd also always wanted to be an actress. And unlike me, she didn't have any problem going after the things she wanted.

The microwave beeped, pulling me out of my reverie. I pulled out the bag, and, not bothering with bowls, headed downstairs.

As expected, Kennedy and Eric were sitting together on the love seat, their arms touching.

"Here," I said, tossing the bag into Kennedy's lap as I slid onto the hard floor.

"Ouch! That's hot!" she yelped.

"Bree!" Eric grabbed the bag. "Sorry, Bree loves hot stuff because she has a freakish internal temperature. She thinks anything below tropical is freezing."

"And you decided to go to school in *Maine*?" Kennedy barely hid her disdain. "Or did your parents just force you here?"

"No one forces me to do anything," I said.

"Except walk through the graveyard." Eric grinned. "Are you superstitious, Kennedy?"

She shook her head. "No. I'm a townie, remember? We're born to be tough. We don't have the luxury of living behind a stone fence like you all do."

Just then, the doorbell rang. Kennedy lurched forward, the popcorn spilling onto the floor in a constellation-like pattern.

"For someone who's not superstitious, you seem pretty jumpy," I noted lightly.

"I'm fine. I was just surprised."

"But you knew people were coming, right?" I pressed. It was the oldest trick in the book: Pretend to have a party, but only invite the guy you like. Even *I* knew that one. I was going to give her a harder time by asking even more questions, until I noticed fear flicker across her face.

"Should I get it?" Eric asked, already sliding off the couch.

"No . . . that's fine." Kennedy leapt to her feet, but Eric followed her. At my feet, Brutus whined.

"I'm coming, too!" I called. I was definitely uneasy.

The three of us formed an odd tableau as Kennedy stood on her tiptoes and peered through the window. I mimicked her motion, recognizing the red-haired kid who'd gotten kicked out of auditions. Zach? Zeke?

"Who is it?" Eric asked.

"Um . . ." Kennedy shifted from side to side. Clearly, she didn't want to open the door. But Eric didn't catch her signals.

"It's that dude from the Trusty Ax," he said, surprised. "Yo, I'm Eric." He held out his hand as he swung open the door.

"Zach. And we met," the red-haired guy said, already looking beyond Eric's shoulder at Kennedy. "Kennedy, we need to talk."

"No, Zach. Not now." Her voice had a pleading edge to it. Zach's jaw tightened. I shifted from one foot to the other, hoping Eric understood what was happening in front of him. But Eric's bemused expression remained the same. "I'm here with MacHale kids. We're *rehearsing*," she added.

"Okay. I don't want to disturb you. But I just want to talk, K? It's important."

"So is this," Kennedy hissed as she slammed the door shut. She turned toward us with a big smile. "Sorry about that! He's just a little . . . not right. You saw what happened at the auditions with him. He's sometimes overemotional."

"Is he dangerous?" Eric asked, taking a protective step toward Kennedy.

"No . . . no." Kennedy shook her head and carefully locked the door. She flicked off the outside light. "Let's go downstairs."

As we followed her, I unsuccessfully tried to make eye contact with Eric. She and that Zach kid must have had a relationship. I was sure of it.

"Anyway, sorry about that!" Kennedy slid back to her spot on the couch.

"So, Zach wasn't invited. . . . Was anyone else?" I pressed.

"Shh!" Kennedy stage-whispered as she pressed her finger to her lips and turned to her laptop. "I want to hear how he does iambic pentameter."

I leaned against the back of the couch. Eric's bare leg was

close to mine. This was going to be a long night. I felt my iPhone wedged in my pocket. Should I Tweet about this?

Technically, yes, I should. But there was no way I wanted to commit this awkward encounter to Internet eternity. At MacHale, it didn't count if it wasn't Tweeted. And I did *not* want this to count.

But something about the way Kennedy had angled her body toward Eric's on the couch made it very obvious that it definitely did.

CHAPTER 9

Skye Henderson
Ready to get in character, starting at the costume closet. Follow along on #machalehamlet to see some exclusive behind-the-scenes images.

Tristan Schuler
Digging up some major dirt on the players in #machalehamlet. You've been warned. . . .

Hamlet's Ghost @hamletsghost
How to describe the end of the first week of rehearsals? Some might say . . . electric. What do you think @alleyesonbree?

"I think you're a drama queen, Tristan," I whispered under my breath, even as I pressed RETWEET on all three.

In the past week, everything Hamlet's Ghost had Tweeted had to do with the actual stars of the show. I learned that Kennedy and Eric had been meeting up before official rehearsals; that Rex Andrews, who played Polonius, had been spotted making out with Leah Banks during a dinner break; and that Skye Henderson had been raiding the costume closet. I felt a twinge at being excluded, but mainly, I felt glad that I was no longer being scrutinized. In fact, I couldn't help but feel that maybe not being in the play was a good thing.

After all, my level had plummeted. I was bored, but maybe being bored was better than being sad, suspicious, and terrified.

For amusement, I'd been watching Skye. She'd heard about the movie-watching "party," and had arrived at rehearsal furious — and followed Eric's and Kennedy's every move. If it didn't hurt so much that Eric wasn't interested in me, it would almost be funny.

Maybe because she was mad at Eric, maybe because hanging around me made her feel better about her own life, or maybe for a combination of reasons only known to Skye, she'd actually become friendlier with me — or at least, friendly-ish. Because we were seemingly the only two people on campus to wake up early enough for dining hall breakfast, we'd seen each other almost every morning. The other day, we'd even sat at the same table, although we'd spent most of the time reading from our respective phones. At one of these breakfasts, she'd asked if I'd noticed Kennedy and Eric getting close, and I'd given her the intel about the *Hamlet*-watching "party" the week before.

But at the end of breakfast, as she was clearing her tray, she'd asked if I would help her with a *Hamlet* project. And because it was early and I hadn't had any caffeine, I'd said yes. And now, it seemed, today was the day. Even Hamlet's Ghost was excited.

I smiled as I realized that could make a good Tweet — and might inspire the Hamlet's Ghost account to actually interact a bit more with *me* and the "official" Hamlet news I Tweeted from my account. It was weird the way Tristan never owned up to the account, even though it *had* to be him. But as long as he'd taken my warning to heart and kept the Tweets focused on anyone else but me, I didn't really care. I quickly typed:

> **Briana Beland** @alleyesonbre
> Even @hamletsghost is excited to see how Ophelia prepares for her part. Can't-miss drama at #machalehamlet.

"Hey, can we order from Salad Shakers tonight? We've done pizza for the past three nights and I'm feeling a little bloated." I glanced up from my phone to see Kennedy was patting her flat stomach in mock concern.

"You know I don't do dinner orders. Ask someone on stage crew," I said, glancing back down at my phone. *What's the point?* We were one week into rehearsals, nothing had happened worth Tweeting about, and watching Kennedy flirt with Eric — and Eric flirt back — was unmitigated torture.

"I don't *know* anyone on stage crew. Besides, I need to block my scene now," Kennedy whined. "Please, can you just pass the order on to whoever's doing it? It would be a really big help to me. Unless you're busy?" The inflection of her voice told me that she definitely didn't think I was.

From the theater entrance, I saw Eric making his way toward us. *Great.* Now I could have a front-row seat to their back-and-forth flirtation, which had only gotten more obvious and more annoying since our weird movie night. I pasted a flat smile on my face, trying to prepare myself for what I was about to see.

"Hey!" Eric sounded like he was in a great mood. And why wouldn't he be? Unlike me, whose entire job was just to sit in the auditorium for every eight-hour rehearsal day, bored to tears while Mr. O'Dell spent hours blocking a single scene, Eric was actually *doing* something the whole time. And when we finally *did* get off for breaks, he was too busy running lines with Kennedy or going over additional notes with Mr. O'Dell to hang out. I'd talked to him less in the past week than I had in the two days surrounding auditions. "My two favorites. How's it going?" Eric asked, draping his arms over both of our shoulders.

I resisted the urge to roll my eyes and wiggle out of his grasp. In the past week, his confidence had become almost annoyingly over-the-top. But that didn't negate the electric surge up my spine when his arm touched my shoulder.

"I'm just trying to order dinner," Kennedy whined.

"Oh. Can we do Kickin' Chicken?"

"But I want salad tonight," Kennedy said with a pout.

"No, it's still vacation. Kickin' Chicken. Please, Bree?" Eric pushed out his lower lip and gave his best puppy-dog expression.

"You're begging? That's so lame!" Kennedy placed her hands on her tiny hips. "Bree, Instagram this. Actors in an argument. It's character work; people would love to see it. And Eric's puppy face is so cute!"

"I have to go order dinner." Better that than watch Kennedy's nauseating display of affection. It wasn't that she was a bad actress. . . . It was that she acted *all the time*. She was even worse than Skye. Her voice was always decibels louder than necessary, she always tossed her curls over her shoulder whenever she laughed, and she automatically turned to her right whenever she even *sensed* a camera in her vicinity. It made me wonder what Mr. O'Dell had been talking about when he'd said *I'd* been inauthentic onstage.

"You okay, Bree?" Eric cocked his head and looked over at me, catching me off guard. I knew my tone sounded less than perky, but I didn't really expect him to actually *listen* to me.

" 'When sorrows come, they come not in single spies, but in batallions,' right?"

"What?" Kennedy asked flatly.

"Act four, Claudius." I scanned the auditorium until my eye fell on Christian Kent, a Forsyth local who always wore a plaid shirt and a blue-knit beanie cap. Claudius was supposed to be the smooth, dangerous uncle who murders Hamlet's father, then sweeps in and marries his mother. The way Christian played him made Claudius seem like the bumbling, black sheep uncle whose only smooth trick is sneaking away from restaurants without paying the bill. I squinted into the darkness, barely able to differentiate his bulky form from the chairs.

"I gotta go." I made my way toward backstage. Just before I headed into the tangle of black curtains, I felt a tap on my shoulder.

"Briana. I have been looking for you *everywhere*! But I didn't want to see that *girl* falling all over Eric. Doesn't she *realize* how pathetic she looks?" Skye shook her head sadly. "And I bet she was asking you to order from Salad Shakers. Don't do it. *No one* likes it. I hate it. And we MacHale ladies have to stick together, right?"

"Sure." I felt a tug of sympathy for Skye. She may have been unaware of how hard she was trying, but no one else was. In the dim light of the single bare bulb that lit up the theater, I could see that her eyes were lined with more dark eyeliner than usual, and the dark red lipstick she had on gave her an almost Goth appearance.

I leaned in to give her a hug, but she pulled away right before I initiated the double-kiss she gave to everyone.

"Sorry, my makeup," she said apologetically. "Anyway, I don't have a lot of scene work today, so I thought this would be the perfect day to really delve into my character. And I want you to Tweet about it. I think it'll be great for people to see how an actress prepares, you know? A *real* actress, not a charity case," she added darkly. "So, I was about to go through the costume cage and find something to wear during the rehearsal. I know it won't be, like, the *same* as what I'll wear onstage, but I feel like wearing some sort of costume will help me become closer to the character. Do you know what I mean?"

"Yup," I said, as though she hadn't already told me.

"Great!" Skye said happily. "Also, your roommate is Willow, right? Do you know what she's planning for costumes? Because I have some ideas. . . ."

"Actors!" Mr. O'Dell strode onstage, his black leather pants swishing with every step. Immediately, everyone, including Skye and me, quieted down and gazed over at him.

"Do I have everyone's attention?" Mr. O'Dell asked unnecessarily. Of course he did. "Good. So, we're done with our first week of rehearsal and finished with blocking all of our key scenes." A smattering of applause broke out, and Mr. O'Dell raised his hand to stop it. "But we still have a long way to go. Now we're going to break down the smaller, more intimate scenes, the ones with only two or three characters, where we really need to find the emotional heart of the action."

My own heart flip-flopped at the word *intimate*. I'd been able to handle watching the large ensemble scenes come together. But now, it would be just Kennedy and Eric, alone together onstage, forced to find their emotional chemistry. And I would be Tweeting their every move. I set my jaw. Better get used to it now.

"We have one more week of all-day rehearsals before school is back in session. Soon, you'll have your peers, your classes, and your other commitments vying for your attention. But this — the stage, your fellow actors, the world of Elsinore Castle — is always number one. Is that clear?"

"Yes," Skye whispered rapturously. I realized I was nodding my own head in agreement. I immediately stopped.

I'm not in the play. It hurt each time I realized that no matter how many hours I spent in the theater, or how many Tweets I wrote, when the curtain went up, it would be them — not me — getting applause. Nothing I Tweeted mattered, not really.

"Good. So today, the plan is to block the Hamlet and the ghost scene. It's got some complicated details, so it's imperative that everyone is on point, paying attention, and taking notes. I need everyone to be playing their A-game. Every minute lost to carelessness etches away at the play's integrity."

Every minute lost to carelessness etches away at the play's integrity. That was good. Quickly, I typed it up, added the hashtag #machalehamlet, then obediently looked up at Mr. O'Dell. His face had a faraway expression, and his gaze was directed above the last row of the auditorium and toward the darkened lighting booth. Once again, it was hard for me to tear my eyes away from him. Presence, a look, whatever it was that he had — I wanted it.

He clapped his hands again, the spell broken. "All right. Places, please."

Skye poked my arm. "Let's go to the costume closet," she hissed as cast members shuffled into their spots.

"Really?" I was surprised that she'd actually disobey Mr. O'Dell.

"Yeah. He won't notice."

Together, the two of us crept through the tangle of black velvet curtains into the chaotic backstage area.

"Come this way," she whispered, as if I didn't know the backstage as well as she did. She climbed up the ten steps to the large metal cage that held rows and rows of costumes, used in more than a century's worth of MacHale theatrical endeavors. As I climbed the stairs, I heard a scream, followed by a flash of light.

And then everything went dark.

"Skye?" I hissed. No answer. All I could hear was Mr. O'Dell's voice projecting from the stage, giving notes on where he wanted Eric to stand.

"Skye?" I asked, louder this time. "This isn't funny."

I heard a weird hum, and then, suddenly, the backstage was illuminated in a dim light.

This time, I screamed.

Lying slumped over on the landing, surrounded by the scattered pages of her highlighted *Hamlet* script, was Skye Henderson. Her body was twisted at an awkward angle and her eyes and mouth were open.

But the worst part of all was the inhuman noise surrounding us. The screaming wouldn't stop. I heard it echoing in my head, above the commotion of people rushing backstage. I knew a crowd was gathering behind me, and the mingling scents of cologne and perfume and fear emanating from the bodies pressing toward me made my stomach lurch. But I couldn't see the crowd. All I saw was blackness, and I wasn't sure if my eyes were open or closed or what was happening around me. I didn't care. I wanted was to get as far away as I could from the sound, which felt like it was coming from the very center of my brain. I held my hands over my ears, startled when I felt a sharp jolt on my shoulders.

Mr. O'Dell held my shoulders in a death grip, almost rocking me back and forth as he glanced up the staircase to Skye's motionless body.

"Stay away," he said roughly. He pushed me aside and sprinted up the stairs and knelt by Skye. But he didn't call her name or try to perform CPR or do any of the things you were supposed to do with a body like that, one that was awkwardly slumped across several steps and that didn't seem to be moving or breathing.

I wanted to throw up. I leaned against the concrete wall, sure I would faint when another set of hands roughly pulled me aside.

"What happened?" It was Eric's voice. He was simultaneously pushing and rubbing my shoulder, and even though I knew it was wrong, I couldn't help but notice how good it felt, and how reassured his grip made me feel.

"I don't know. She fell. Or she tripped. And then . . . there was the light and then the scream. . . . I don't know." My whole body started to tremble, even though I was hot all over, my skin feeling red and raw. He glanced toward Skye and bit his lip.

"We need to call 9-1-1," he announced unnecessarily, as he yanked me toward Mr. O'Dell's office. I nodded mutely. How could he speak? It was as if language had stopped in my brain, my mind only filled with images, each one worse than the last.

The flash of light. The scream. Skye's lifeless body.

"9-1-1, what's your emergency?" I could hear the cool voice on the other end of the line, sounding like it was coming from underwater as it leaked through the receiver. "Hello?" The voice had taken a more urgent edge. I gulped, tasting the sharp, sour smell of bile in my throat. I was going to get sick. I clutched Eric's arm tightly.

"Hi," Eric said. "I'm at the theater at MacHale, and there's been an accident. I think. I mean, I don't know what happened, but someone's really hurt. . . . I don't know if she's alive."

My knees buckled.

"What do you mean?" I croaked. Eric waved his hand toward me, as if to brush me away. I shut my eyes again.

"We're at 1101 Old Church Lane. MacHale. Yup. It seems that there was an electrical accident. I'm not sure if she's breathing. No one touched her. All right. All right. Yes." Eric hung up, but kept his hand on the receiver. We didn't look at each other. I could hear his breathing, heavy and ragged, but I couldn't see his expression, which made me feel even more alone.

The commotion outside the office was deafening, especially the high-pitched shrieks of one girl that I could hear above everything else. I just wanted her to be quiet. If she was quiet, then everything would be okay. It didn't make sense, but nothing else did.

I opened my mouth to ask Eric to *please* try to get that girl, whoever it was, to shut up, when I realized I couldn't.

Because the endless, relentless screams weren't coming from anyone else.

They were coming from me.

Eric cupped his hands over my shoulders and shook me hard. "Just breathe, all right? Can you do that? Breathe in for five seconds, out for five seconds. . . . Do you hear me? Do it for Skye." Eric's voice was low and hypnotic. Was he kidding? How could I breathe when Skye may or may not have been dead? And what did he mean when he'd said there was an *electrical accident*? But even as my brain protested, my body calmed down. Soon, the sound of our breathing was joined by the wail of police sirens and the lower-pitched blare of the fire truck. After my horrible screams, the sirens sounded almost musical. I tugged on Eric's sleeve to tell him how pretty I thought it sounded, aware that I must be in shock to even think that, when the door swung open.

"You two alone in here?" A fireman glanced around.

"Yes. We're the ones who called, sir," Eric said.

"You two need to get out. Now. We're evacuating the theater. Electrical problem. We don't know what's safe," one said gruffly, pushing Eric aside.

Electrical.

Like the Tweet. *Hamlet's Ghost.* Tristan.

"Eric," I gulped, my mouth dry. But before I could finish the sentence, he grabbed my wrist and pulled me outside, where I was greeted by a shock of cold air. I'd left my coat in the auditorium.

"Listen to me. What did you see?" Eric's eyes were wide and he kept licking his lips. He was terrified.

"Hamlet's Ghost . . ." I began, trying to form my thoughts in a way that made sense.

"*Bree!*" Eric snapped. He clamped his hands on my shoulders. But his touch wasn't the rough, sensitive one I'd spent the last weeks craving. "Don't be insane. Skye is really hurt. Just tell me what happened."

His voice broke. Just then, Kennedy bounded over to us, threw her arms around Eric, and began sobbing against his shoulder. Eric let go of me, and I stumbled backwards a few steps.

I couldn't stay here. Not with Eric glancing at me with suspicion. Not with the image of Skye's lifeless body embedded in my brain.

The doors opened and four paramedics rushed past us. Skye was on a stretcher, her face covered with an oxygen mask. The dark red lipstick she'd been wearing looked like blood, especially against her pale face.

"She's alive!" a voice called from the crowd. I whirled around. It was Christian, aka Claudius.

"How do you know?" I heard a Forsyth girl ask.

Christian's eyes widened, as if he'd only just realized he'd spoken out loud and that everyone was now staring at him. "I don't, really," he confessed. "It's just that she had an oxygen mask on. They wouldn't give that to someone who was dead. I mean, right?"

Another fireman walked out of the building, trailed by Mr. O'Dell. Mr. O'Dell looked pale and shaky, following the fireman like a lost puppy.

"Students?" the fireman said gruffly, as Mr. O'Dell mutely stood by his side. "Go back to your dorms. You'll be apprised of the situation on a need-to-know basis. The premises is not safe until we've inspected it thoroughly."

"Will she be all right?" Leah Banks asked in a small voice.

The fireman's eyes flicked up toward the sky, the same automatic gesture I did whenever I made a wish. "Let's hope so." He turned on his heel. As he did, I elbowed my way past people, dimly hearing "Stop" and "Is she okay?" called as I ran past, but I didn't care. I couldn't stand there a second longer. I ran as if my brain were separated from my body, past Scholar's Walk and into the woods. It was only there, far away from the theater, that I felt it was safe to stop. I rested my hands on my knees and breathed heavily. I could taste blood rising in my throat. A crow cawed in the distance. Above me, the pale, full moon gleamed down on me.

I thought of those two phantom eyes I'd thought I'd seen in the forest, that night before auditions. If I squinted, I could still see them. I thought I'd been terrified that night, but I'd had no idea what real terror was. Terror was seeing someone lying face up, their gaze unfocused and blank. Terror was knowing danger surrounded you, but there was nothing you could do to stop it. And terror was knowing that even if I didn't know where, or who, he was, that Hamlet's Ghost would certainly be on my Twitter feed when I got back to my dorm.

CHAPTER 10

Briana Beland @alleyesonbree

The entire #machalehamlet cast hopes that Skye gets better as soon as possible. Love and thoughts are with her.

Tristan Schuler

Let's play a game! Any guesses on who @hamletsghost will kill next? My guess is it won't be @alleyesonbree. . . .

I slammed my laptop shut with a bang as I struggled to catch my breath. Was Tristan insinuating that *I'd* killed Skye? I knew that he liked to joke, but *this* wasn't funny. As soon as I'd gotten back to the dorm, I'd deleted everything of @hamletsghost's that I'd ever Retweeted. But not before it had been Retweeted five times, mostly by people I didn't know. Even more disconcerting was the amount of followers I had gained — eighty-seven since the accident. But deleting the Tweets didn't make me feel any better. It wasn't like I was deleting @hamletsghost.

Willow jumped at the sound of my laptop lid closing. "Are you okay?" she asked. She was lying on her bed, barely visible in the shadowy candlelight that dimly lit up our dorm room. Until the entire MacHale electrical system was investigated, the school had cut the electricity on campus as a precaution, making us entirely dependent on the candles that we weren't supposed to have in our dorms. Even worse was that we were being forced to remain in our rooms, making the accident seem even more surreal and scary. No one knew what was going on. People's battery power had obviously dwindled; only a few people were actively Facebooking and Tweeting. My own phone battery was on red, dangerously close to dying out entirely.

"Yeah . . . just jumpy."

She nodded. "So, what are you going to do?"

"What do you mean?" I asked.

"Like, now . . ." She watched me closely, and I squirmed under her gaze.

"I don't know. Hang out, I guess. Wait for news. Have you heard from Tad?" Tad was one of the few juniors on campus who had a car, and he'd driven Eric to the hospital. I imagined Eric leaning over Skye's bed. I guess that she'd finally gotten his attention.

"No. He and Eric are still at the hospital. You know, people have been asking me about you."

My skin prickled. "What do you mean?"

"Just . . . what you're like, who you're friends with, what you do . . . It's weird, I never really thought of you as the mysterious type or anything, but when I thought about it, I realized that I don't know very much about you at all."

My breath came in shallow spurts. I knew she wasn't accusing me. She was just making an observation. But I couldn't help but feel there was something dark below the surface. "Do *you* have any questions for me?" I asked. *Do you think I did it?*

Willow shook her head. "Not really. I don't really believe in gossip. I'm just saying that you should be careful."

"Okay." I lifted the lid of my laptop. The battery icon in the upper right hand of the screen had just turned red, a sure sign that my power was about to die. I shut my laptop again, more gently this time.

Willow turned to face me. She scrunched her nose. "What do you think about dying?"

"What?!" I exclaimed. Then I noticed that she was toying with a box of hair color. "Oh. You mean hair dye. I feel like I've already done enough damage." I squinted at myself in the mirror, the flickering candlelight on my reflection only making my orange hair more garish.

"I mean, we might as well, right? Nothing left to lose. It'll give us something to do."

"Right. Something to do," I echoed. I had a strange sensation that Willow was trying to keep an eye on me. But who would do that? Was she taking it on herself because she thought I might be a serial killer, or had someone else told her that I needed to be watched?

She held up the hair-dye box again. "What do you think?"

"I guess it's fine."

"Good!" She began gathering supplies as I tried to ignore the hammering in my heart.

"Come on," Willow urged. As we turned the corner to the communal bathroom, Sabrina Stokes, a sophomore on stage crew, gave me the side eye.

"You guys look like you're having a spa party," she said suspiciously, referencing the common practice of communal makeovers during procrastination-fueled evenings. "Don't you think that's a little insensitive? I mean, Skye just died."

"What?" The hair-dye box Willow had asked me to carry thunked to the floor.

"I just heard from Jenny. Her mom works at Forsyth General."

"Oh," I said in a small voice as my brain raced to process the information. Despite the horror of the scene, I'd been convinced she'd pull through, that she be back at school in a few days, relishing in all the attention that came with a near-death experience. It'd be her finest moment.

"But I guess you knew that already, didn't you?" Sabrina asked, her voice laced with suspicion. Before I could respond, she continued padding down the hall.

I stared at the box of hair dye on the floor.

Dead. How was that possible? I felt like I should cry or scream, but I couldn't. It was too surreal.

Willow turned toward me, shock stamped on her face.

"What do we do now?" I asked. My voice was oddly stilted, as if my brain needed to reboot in between each word.

"I don't know." Willow reached down and picked up the box of hair dye. "I guess . . . let's just do this. I mean, we don't *really* know yet. Maybe Jenny doesn't have all the information. And I think it's good to do something."

"Okay." I wanted to go back to my room and check to see if anyone had Tweeted or texted, but I also didn't want to be alone.

Willow and I didn't talk as she dyed my hair, and I don't think she noticed the tears dripping from my face while my head was dunked in the sink. But when we were done, I felt a tiny bit better. At least I wasn't alone.

As I entered the doorway I noticed her discreetly pull her phone out of her pocket, the light from the screen creating a rectangle on her black jeans.

I walked over to my desk to check on my laptop. The sleep-indicator light on my laptop was still blinking on and off, like a lighthouse beacon. I was surprised it still had power. I jostled the mouse track pad as the screen reopened back on my Twitter feed. Only a few Tweets had shown up on my feed since the last time I checked; it was clear that most people were out of battery power.

Except for Hamlet's Ghost.

> **Hamlet's Ghost** @hamletsghost
> Seems the "sky writing" is clear: We need another Ophelia u/s for #machalehamlet. Seems to me it should go to @alleyesonbree. But do you agree?

My hands turned clammy.

"So, um, I'm supposed to head to a party now. . . . Do you want to come with me?" Willow asked from her side of the room.

"A party? Tonight?"

Willow nodded, but her gaze darted around the room and she wouldn't make eye contact.

"Sure, I guess so?" Was she actually extending a real invitation or an invite out of pity? And why was she acting so weird? I felt like an awkward younger sister she'd been forced to babysit. "But I'm also fine staying by myself."

"*No,*" Willow said vehemently. "You need to come. Seriously."

"Okay, I guess . . . I mean, if that's what everyone is doing." At least I'd be able to hear what had *really* happened to Skye. "But what about the lockdown thing?"

"There are ways to get around *that*," she said mysteriously.

Normally, I'd be thrilled to be invited to a secret MacHale party. But not tonight. Not with Skye's body lying cold and still in some hospital bed. Or worse, the morgue. I winced as terrible images flooded my mind.

"Actually, I think I'll stay. I'm not in the mood."

Willow stopped mid-brush and shook her head. "No, you have to come. What are you going to do *here*, by *yourself*?"

"Just . . ." I sighed. "Okay. Fine."

"Good." Willow was moving quickly and nervously, knocking her cosmetics against one another.

"Are you okay?" I finally asked.

"Yeah. Great. Let's go!" She said in a high voice as she stared at me intently.

To avoid her weird gaze, I glanced at my reflection. The shade Willow had chosen brought out the caramel color around the iris of my eyes that my mom had always sworn was there, but I had never seen myself. I was wearing a fleece and jeans, just like I'd been for the last week, the uniform of the just-trying-to-blend-in MacHale kids on break. I didn't look like Ophelia anymore. But I no longer looked unhinged, the way I had with my post-audition orange hair.

"By the way, people will probably be upset about Skye so just . . . be cool."

"What do you mean?" I bristled. Wasn't I just as upset as anyone?

"Just . . . I know you want to be Ophelia and I know you like Eric, but just keep that stuff on the DL."

"I don't *talk* about that stuff!"

"Right." Willow puffed her cheeks out as she exhaled. "I'm sorry. I know you don't. It's just . . . Don't take this the wrong way, but sometimes, I feel like you just . . ." She trailed off.

"Sometimes I just what?" I pressed.

"You just play up the victim thing. I mean, I know today sucked. But it's like everything is all about *you*. I mean, that's even your Twitter handle, right? I'm just saying, some things aren't all about Bree."

"I know that," I said quietly.

"Good." Willow opened the door to the corridor, glancing left and right before stepping over the threshold. "And I *do* believe you," she added meaningfully.

"Believe me about what?" I asked. But she didn't respond. Instead, she turned down the hallway, heading to the basement steps.

I'd been to the basement exactly once, on the new-resident tour on the first day of fall semester. Occasionally used as a multipurpose gathering room, the basement was overlooked by the Rockefeller girls in favor of hanging out in the parlor, which had a flat-screen TV and plenty of floor-to-ceiling windows that gave a picturesque view of Daniels Pond. The basement smelled weird; had a carpet that our tour guide had told us we should always wear shoes on, without specifying why; and didn't have any WiFi. When it was used at all, it tended to be by seniors desperately trying to write their theses without distraction. But just like everything else at MacHale, the basement held secrets, too.

Willow flicked on the lights and grabbed the edge of the carpet, yanking it to the side of the room. A few objects I *hoped* were dust motes and not insects flew up my nose and caused me to sneeze. Underneath the carpet were filthy wooden floorboards surrounding a large metal grate. She leaned down and pulled on the grate, which lifted up easily.

"That looks like a death trap," I joked. I cringed when I heard the words in my ears.

Willow blinked her large Bambi-like eyes at me. *"Bree,"* she said, her voice gently chiding, as though I were a toddler who'd broken free of her mother's hand to run ahead. "Do not get weird. I'm on your side. And you don't need to be afraid of *this*. It used to be part of the heating system or something, but they got rid of that years ago. Now it's just a straight drop into the tunnels," she said, as if she were describing something as straightforward as a shortcut to the dining hall.

"They don't show this on the brochure," I said nervously as I gazed into the darkness of the hole in front of me. "You *are* going first, right?"

"Of course. I promise you have *nothing* to worry about. It's like a trapdoor. We've done it a lot of times. And it's not, like, a *drop* drop. No one's ever gotten hurt."

"So what do you do about all this?" I gestured to the disarray surrounding us.

She shrugged and wiped a dark smudge from her cheek. "Well, that depends. During the school year, we usually pay Robert to cover for us and say he's, like, exterminating or whatever," she said, naming the groundskeeper who constantly roamed the campus. I'd occasionally seen him muttering to himself while standing near the pond, and I'd always steered clear. "Anyway, we can't do that today because he's on break, so we'll just leave it and hope no one sees it while we're gone." Willow edged herself off the side and into the opening. Seconds later, I heard a soft thud.

"Come on!" she called, her voice faint and echoey.

I perched on the edge and dangled my legs into the darkness. I felt like I did when I was a kid and learning how to swim, when my mom had pushed me into the water. I remembered sputtering, trying to breathe, feeling the liquid all around me. I'd finally kicked my way to the surface when I felt two strong hands underneath my armpits.

"What were you doing?" Dad had yelled angrily.

"She needed to get out of her head," Mom had replied. "See, she's fine when she doesn't think."

I hadn't been fine. As soon as my father had hoisted me back up onto the pool deck, I'd burst into tears and hadn't stopped crying for hours.

"Bree, come on!" Willow called from the darkness.

Don't think. I squeezed my eyes shut and pushed myself over the edge.

I landed on my knees with a thud.

"Ow." I winced as I stood up, realizing that I'd landed on the same knee that I'd skinned in the woods the other night.

Willow reached to grab my hand and pulled me to my feet. I blinked in the semi-darkness. Mismatched pieces of furniture were jumbled everywhere, and a large cage surrounded a boiler in the center of the room. I cringed and backed away. It reminded me too much of the costume cage.

Willow seemed oblivious. "Every building on campus is connected. "Which, of course, *they* don't want us to know. Unless you know how to work the system."

"How did you learn about this?" My heart stopped pounding. When Willow had mentioned an underground tunnel, I'd imagined a pitch-black maze, a sort of corollary to the creepy cemetery on the other side of campus. But this just seemed like long-forgotten storage space. Farther down the corridor, I could see dusty graduation gowns hanging from metal clothing racks.

"I found out about it from Heather McKay. . . . She was a senior when I was a freshman. But it's not like *everyone* goes down to the tunnels. It's sort of, like, a specific group."

"Like a secret society?" I asked.

"No. Not like a secret society," Willow said coldly.

"Sorry." I knew we were both on edge, but I also couldn't understand why she was being so mean all of a sudden. I weighed my options. It'd be better to go to the party than hang out in the room by myself. *Especially* if I was already feeling weird and antsy.

I took off behind Willow. Five steps later, I found myself engulfed in a swath of shapeless black fabric. I twisted, getting more and more caught until my shin banged against something hard. I heard the clank of metal.

"Help!" I called. And then I felt the fabric whoosh over my head. I felt a blast of musty basement air against my face.

I blinked in the candlelight. I was standing in the middle of a rack of shapeless black graduation gowns. *Those* had been my captors.

Twenty yards away from us, the hallway came to a T-shaped intersection. A couch and a few chairs were scattered in the area, illuminated by a few pillar candles precariously placed on the cracked concrete floor. I squinted. I could see Tad and

Chad, as well as a few girls from the *Hamlet* cast. They all gazed at me curiously, and I realized each of them was holding a small votive candle.

"Hey guys. I brought Bree," Willow said unnecessarily.

I perched next to Vivy Brownslee, a Forsyth student who played Getrude in the play.

"Hey," I whispered.

"So are you happy now?" she whispered back as she scooted away from me.

"What do you mean?"

"Skye." She jerked her candle forward, illuminating an eight-by-ten photograph of Skye; a blown-up picture of her Twitter avatar. The photo was angled so it seemed her gaze was directly at me. "Everyone says that means you'll be the understudy *and* get to play Ophelia during matinees. Seems lucky."

"Luck or . . ." Tristan said as he joined our conversation. His dark eyes flashed. "How do you feel about Skye?" he asked calmly. Chad and Tad hulked behind him, making me feel like I was on a trial without a jury. I looked around, only to be confronted by a dozen pairs of angry eyes.

"I'm devastated, of course. What do you think?"

"You know she's dead," Tristan said.

I nodded. "I heard."

"So we decided to have a vigil for her. We thought it was a good way for us to start the healing process," Tristan explained. I glared mutinously at him. What was he talking about, "healing process"? That wasn't the way Tristan talked. And he sounded like *I* was the one who'd killed her. Anger bubbled inside me, threatening to explode.

"You'd know a lot about healing rituals, wouldn't you, Hamlet's Ghost?"

"Not now, Bree. Remember what we talked about?" Willow asked, a plaintive note in her voice.

"I know what we talked about. And *I'm* talking about the fact that Tristan is *clearly* the one Tweeting . . . and maybe even killing."

Tad lunged toward me.

"Tad. Dude. Lighten up. I've got her under control." Tristan sprang between us.

"What's going on?" I glanced from Tristan to Vivy to Willow. No one would look at me. And then, slowly and horribly, everything dawned on me. People thought *I* was the murderer. People thought that I was Tweeting from the Hamlet's Ghost account. People thought I killed Skye.

"You don't . . . I'm not . . ." I gasped. "Guys, please. Believe me."

"So I guess the real question is, who do you think did it?" Tristan asked calmly.

It felt like the room's temperature had suddenly dropped ten degrees. He also didn't think it was an accident. "Did it? What do you mean?"

"I mean, accidents like that don't just happen, right?" Tristan said. "Skye wasn't an idiot. Not like Andi. And I think it's pretty easy to connect the dots."

"Connect the dots to *who*? To me?" I exploded. "Do you think I *killed* Skye?"

The room had quieted. I could hear the hiss of the radiator in the far-off corner. The lights flickered on the wall. Everyone's head swiveled toward me. No one seemed to be breathing except me, my sharp gasps matching the staccato beat of my heart.

"Seriously?" I exploded. "You think *I killed* Skye Henderson?"

I saw a few shadows nodding yes, but I couldn't make out individual faces.

"I didn't say that," Tristan said calmly. "But I know that *someone* did. And I'm going to find out who."

"Good luck playing detective. I won't stop you. And I'm leaving!" I turned on my heel and ran, hurtling past the graduation gowns, running faster and faster on my way back to Rockefeller. It wasn't until I reached the grate opening that I realized one serious problem. *The grate.* It was one thing to have jumped down, but Willow had never explained how someone climbed back up.

"Bree!" A voice echoed in the hallway.

Tristan.

"Are you kidding?" I hissed.

He held his hands up.

"Bree. It's okay. I just want to talk to you. Alone."

Alone.

I was trapped. I gazed up at the grate, three feet above my head. I was just barely able to graze the edge with my fingers. I looked around for a chair or a ladder, but of course there wasn't one. At least not one I could find. If Willow were here, I had no doubt she'd know exactly how to get back up.

I took a deep breath and jumped.

And then fell to the ground with a thud.

"Ow!" I winced in agony.

"Bree, it's okay." Tristan knelt beside me. "It's okay."

"Why should I trust you?" My voice rose into a sob. "I *hate* you."

"No. Bree. For the last time, I'm *not* Hamlet's Ghost . . . and I don't think you are, either. But you want to be an actress, right? You want the spotlight on you? Well, for the next week, you have it. For your own good, and for everyone else's, you *need* people to think you're Hamlet's Ghost."

"Why? So you have a story?"

Tristan's face darkened. "Yes. But not the reason you think. I know you think I'm being a bad friend, and I *am*. I know that. I'll make it up to you. But for right now, everyone thinks you're Hamlet's Ghost. And that's much better than the alternative."

"Which is?"

"I can't explain it yet. I need to do research. And it's going to be explosive. But listen to me when I tell you that it's *safest* for people to think you're a murderer."

"Safe for who? Not for me!" My voice rose an octave. I knew MacHale had rituals I didn't understand and traditions I just went along with, but this was absurd. I couldn't *pretend* to be a murderer. I couldn't pretend to Tweet people's deaths. And I couldn't control a Twitter handle that wasn't mine. "Do you mean it's safe for you to spread rumors? I don't know what you're doing or who you are, but it's sick!"

"Trust me, I know what's going on. And you're in danger."

"Trust me, I *know* that. Which is why I want to *get away from you*."

Tristan clamped his fingers around my wrists. "I don't want to hurt you."

"Then *get your hands off me*," I shrieked.

My eyes darted to the door. Tristan followed my gaze. Then, he slowly took off his purple cashmere scarf and draped it around my neck. "I know you're going to run away. But it's cold outside. Consider this a peace offering."

The fabric felt heavy and tight against my neck. I squirmed under its weight.

"You haven't left yet," Tristan noted.

"Could you *please* just tell me what's going on in a way that makes sense?" I shivered and pulled the scarf closer around my body.

Tristan hesitated, then shook his head. "Not yet. Just follow my lead, and you'll be fine. But just know that Hamlet's Ghost is hiding in plain sight. And for the next few days, I want you to just play the role of a lifetime and trust me that I am fixing everything."

"So you want me to just act like a cold-blooded killer. Got that," I said sarcastically.

Tristan sighed again. "I can't tell you anything else. Go. Use that door. But I promise everything will be fine."

"You think I believe your promises? And I'm not going to let you and your stupid quest for drama ruin *my* reputation. Or ruin the show," I added.

I pushed the door, surprised by how light it was. A gust of cold air hit me and I realized this led straight outside. I hurried up the five concrete steps that led from the basement exit to the gas lamp–lit path connecting the dorms.

I could see the towering spires of Rockefeller across from me. It was so close. We never locked our dorm window; it'd be easy to crawl in. All I had to do was get there.

If I ran for it, there was a chance I could be found and stopped, either by one of the roving security guards on campus or by one of the house monitors on their way back from the faculty meeting.

A tree branch cracked, and I started.

Another crack, followed by a scuffle in the snow-covered hedges that fenced the dorm.

"Tristan! This is *not funny*!" I shrieked. Nothing. My fingers inched inside my pocket and clutched my phone. Which was dead. My throat tightened. "Help!" I called in a small voice.

"Hey."

I gasped.

"Whoa. Shh! It's fine. Sorry." A red-haired guy walked out of the shadows and toward me. I stood frozen in place. Zach.

"Oh. Hi." I shifted awkwardly.

"Bree. Just looking for the party. Do you know where it is?"

"Um. It's not really a party."

A shadow crossed his face."Well, I wasn't exactly coming to celebrate."

My knees were shaking. What was he doing here? I remembered the way Kennedy had slammed the door in his face, the way he'd been so defensive around Eric the night of the auditions. I knew nothing about him. But part of me didn't want him to leave.

"Is Tristan there?"

"What?" I asked, caught off guard.

"Tristan. Is he at the party?"

"Why do you want to know?"

Zach opened his mouth as if he were about to say something, then closed it and shook his head. "No reason." He turned and ambled off into the darkness, his boots crunching in the snow.

"Wait!" I called. I knew how Zach saw me. As a spoiled rich girl who didn't like townies. But he *didn't* see me as the murderer. I could tell in his eyes, the way he'd actually looked at me, instead of anywhere else but my face.

"Yeah?" He turned around.

"He's probably in his dorm. Burnside. On the other side of the pond."

"Burnside," Zach repeated. "Got it. Thanks, Bree."

"Yup," I whispered in the darkness. My teeth chattered together and I wished that Eric was there to laugh. The single light from the room at the top of Taylor Hall flicked off. It was a sign that the faculty meeting had ended, and that I had to move, fast.

Ready, set, go. I forced one foot in front of the other and sprinted toward our window, which was thankfully open an inch, despite the subzero weather, courtesy of Willow's forgetfulness. I hooked my knee over the window ledge and tumbled down on Willow's bed, causing a flurry of snow to dust on the black comforter.

I shut the window and lit a few of Willow's candles, casting the room into a dim amber light. My heart thudded against my chest. I whirled around to look out the window, wondering if I was being watched. The entire campus was dark, making it impossible to see beyond the snow-capped Rockefeller hedgerows. No one was there.

I looked back at my laptop screen, at the red battery icon,

signaling only minutes of power. Not now. I couldn't deal with this now. I slammed down the laptop cover. Then I locked the windows, as well as the door.

A few weeks ago, I'd wondered what it would be like to be Ophelia, unsure if the madness that surrounded her was coming from everyone around her, or inside her own mind.

But now I didn't have to pretend. Because that was exactly how I already felt now, in my own, very real life. And unlike Ophelia, I didn't have a script — or a clue to how everything would end.

CHAPTER 11

Briana Beland @alleyesonbree
Trivia time! Who, on campus, has, in the words of Hamlet, "a vicious mole of nature in them?" (A certain streaky-haired #machale supersleuth, mayhap?)

Tristan Schuler
Really @alleyesonbree? Tweeting insults is a little bit low, don't you think? Or are you saying you're ready to get dirty?

Briana Beland @alleyesonbree
No, I'm saying that you should spend less time chasing rumors and more time studying Shakespeare. That's all.

I scrolled down my feed, disappointed Tristan hadn't responded. The lights had come on in the middle of the night, waking me up and making the party/vigil/whatever it was seem especially dreamlike.

I stretched in bed. We had rehearsals at nine. Or rather, were supposed to have had rehearsals at nine. I wasn't sure if they were going to go on in light of the tragedy.

I swung my legs out of bed. As I was gathering my shower stuff, the sharp ringing of our in-room phone startled me. Since we always used our cell phones, the campus phone hardly *ever* rang. Even advisors knew to text or e-mail us about appointments.

"Hello?" I answered curiously.

"Ms. Beland?" Mr. O'Dell's smooth voice emanated through the receiver.

"Yes?"

"Can you come to my office, please? I wanted to talk to you before rehearsal starts."

"Before rehearsal?" I repeated.

"Yes, before rehearsal," Mr. O'Dell said brusquely. "First rule of show business: The show must go on."

"Right." I didn't even try to guess what he was talking about.

"See you in five minutes, then?" It wasn't a question.

"Yes, sir."

Four and a half minutes later, and I'd raced my unshowered self down to the theater. I pushed against the metal backstage door, wincing as I remembered a motionless, unblinking Skye being carried out on a stretcher.

"Mr. O'Dell?" I called. Odd chanting music played softly, making the empty backstage area feel especially eerie. "Mr. O'Dell?" I called again.

"Ophelia!"

I jumped. Mr. O'Dell leaned over the railing of the upper loft, smiling down at me.

"I'm sorry to have scared you." He gave me a small smile. "I was just in the middle of doing my morning meditation. Meditation is *essential* for a serious artist. Do you agree?"

I nodded wordlessly as my overtaxed brain strained to figure out why he'd called me Ophelia. Was he playing some mind game with me?

"Come up, then," he said.

I gingerly climbed the wooden steps, all too aware they were the last steps Skye had ever taken. Mr. O'Dell watched my every move. Once I'd reached the loft platform, he nodded once and motioned for me to follow him into his office.

"Sit." He nodded toward a single metal folding chair opposite his computer.

"So, you've heard the news about Skye."

"Yes . . . it's awful. I'm so sorry."

"Yes, a tragedy," he said more quickly than I might have expected. "And you know it means we have to make alternate arrangements. Skye wouldn't want her death to be in vain. She'd want the show to go on. We'll have her picture in the lobby, and we'll dedicate the performance to her. She'll be remembered forever. In a way, her death was the role of a lifetime. Don't you agree?"

I nodded, even though my brain spun, trying to process what he said. He hadn't known Skye at all. None of us had. But he'd still understood her desire for the spotlight against all odds. And even though his assessment of her death was twisted, it was also true. Skye would have *loved* the attention. I shivered.

"We're all actors here, Briana. 'Life's but a walking shadow, a poor player that struts and frets his hour upon the stage.' " He turned toward me. "*Macbeth*."

"I know." I twisted my fingers in my lap. This conversation was getting seriously bizarre.

"Skye's hour onstage is now eternal. Everyone will remember her. Just like Sarah Charonne."

My body involuntarily shivered at the mention of Sarah's name.

Mr. O'Dell chuckled softly. "Well, this is getting morose. I'll cut to the chase. I want you to understudy for Ophelia and play the part at the matinee. Can you do that?"

My throat felt dry. *Of course* I could do that. But now? And in these circumstances?

Mr. O'Dell's eyes narrowed at my hesitation. "Is there a problem?"

"It's just . . ." I trailed off. What could I say? That there was a weird Twitter account that was predicting deaths? That people thought I was behind it?

"Just what?" Mr. O'Dell prodded.

"Nothing." I plastered on a smile. "Thank you for the opportunity," I said as I scraped my chair back and headed toward the door.

"Of course. I know you're going to kill it."

I turned back sharply, but Mr. O'Dell seemed unaware of how close his comment cut to the bone.

As I headed down the stairs, I spotted Eric sitting on the ancient green couch that took up almost half of the backstage area.

"Eric!" I called.

He looked up and my heart clenched. He looked awful. Stubble covered his paler-than-usual cheeks. His eyes were bloodshot. His gray MacHale sweatshirt had a coffee stain on the front. And instead of his usual shorts, he was wearing a pair of light blue hospital scrubs. "What are you doing here?" His ragged voice was full of disdain.

"I'm . . . nothing. I just was talking to Mr. O'Dell. I'm so sorry about Skye."

"I bet you are," he spat.

His words thudded against my chest, knocking the air out of my lungs. Did Eric really think I'd been involved in Skye's death? How could he? After all the time we'd spent together, he really thought I was capable of *murder*?

Eric's eyes bore into me, defying me to respond. I opened my mouth, ready to proclaim my innocence, but the words never came. Instead, I sighed and looked away.

"Anyway, if you ever need to talk . . . I'm around."

Eric grunted, then turned back down to his phone. I headed toward the front of the theater, feeling more confused and lonely than ever.

CHAPTER 12

Leah Banks

Going to miss Skye so much. So happy to remember her at a chapel vigil.

Kennedy Clifford

Very, very sad day for Forsyth and for MacHale. My thoughts and love are with the remaining member of Riled Up.

I lay facedown on my bed. I knew there was an official vigil in the chapel, but there was no way I could deal with everyone staring at me accusingly. Instead, I kept obsessively refreshing my Twitter feed. Most everyone at MacHale was Tweeting memories of Skye. Very few were mentioning me.

And Tristan was visibly absent.

Finally, I turned my phone off and powered down my computer. I pulled out my thumbed-through copy of *Hamlet.* Maybe the chapel vigil would help people realize that Skye's death was the result of a stupid electrical accident.

Just then, the door banged open. Willow walked through, clad in black tights, a tiny black dress, and a small black hat. A black lace veil dipped over one of her eyes.

I turned toward her and propped my head on my hand. "Hey," I said.

"What did you do?" she asked as she reached over and yanked my phone from my hand.

"Hey!"

"This isn't on," she said accusingly.

"I know. Why do you care?"

"Because of what you Tweeted. Don't you realize that it's not funny? People are really freaking out." She widened her eyes. Her voice didn't sound unfriendly, exactly. Instead, it sounded terrified. And that scared me more than anything.

"What do you mean?"

She went to her own computer and pulled up Twitter. Even though she never used it, she still had an account. It didn't take her long to find the Tweet she was looking for.

> **Hamlet's Ghost** @hamletsghost
> As Shakespeare says, death is a fearful thing. At least for those still living . . . Any ideas who may be next to feel no fear?

"I didn't write that. I *wouldn't* write that. You can look on my computer if you want. . . . I don't have anything. I didn't write it!" The words poured out of my mouth, my voice growing louder and higher pitched with every word.

Willow turned to me, her eyes large and unblinking. "I'm going to stay with Vanessa tonight. You understand, right?"

I stared at her. Vanessa had been Willow's roommate last year. From the little Willow had told me, they'd never gotten along, with Vanessa hating Willow's go-with-the-flow bohemian attitude and penchant for spontaneous room redecoration.

Without waiting for a response, Willow gathered her clothes

from her dresser and flung them into a tote bag. She glanced over her shoulder as she left.

"I know it sucks that you didn't get the part you wanted, but don't take it out on us, okay? We're not the enemies."

The door closed with a soft thud.

A wave of anger crashed over me as I refreshed my Twitter feed. The creepy Hamlet's Ghost Tweet was getting Retweeted rapidly, and since it *wasn't my account*, there wasn't anything I could do to stop it. The only person who could stop it was the one who'd made it.

Tristan.

I squeezed my eyes shut. I couldn't stomach the thought of speaking to him now. But I couldn't let him keep Tweeting. I didn't think he was responsible for Andi and Skye's deaths, not really, but whatever was going on, it had to stop.

I pulled on my coat and hurried out into darkness, ignoring the few kids who were walking from the chapel to the dining hall. I couldn't remember eating anything today, but I wasn't hungry.

I headed toward Burnside, waiting in the shadows of the entryway until a hoodie-wearing kid swiped in. I followed him, hurrying toward Tristan's dorm room.

As I lifted my fist to knock on the door, I heard voices emanating from inside the room. I pressed my ear to the wood.

"Haven't heard from him. He didn't check his mailbox today." It sounded like Tad's slow drawl.

"You gonna let them know?" a slightly lower voice asked.

"I don't know. I don't want him to get mad. You know how Tristan rolls."

There was a short laugh, the nervous *heh-heh* type where nothing is really that funny.

"But, dude, he left his laptop. He'd never leave his laptop."

"I'll figure it out, man."

I'd heard enough. I tiptoed down the hallway, flinching every time my foot landed on a creaky board. Once I'd snuck out of Burnside, I burst into a sprint.

Tristan was missing. Tristan was missing.

The sentence repeated, mantra-like, in my brain until I swiped into Rockefeller.

"Tristan is missing!" I said out loud.

But the parlor was empty and the dorm was silent.

Of course.

People would listen to a fake avatar, but they wouldn't listen to the *real me*. After all, wasn't Tristan's absence proof of his guilt? His words floated to my mind: *Hamlet's Ghost is hiding in plain sight.*

Well, where was he, then?

CHAPTER 13

Scott Eichner

Man, wish I'd sat this Winterm out. Heard the new girl @alleyesonbree is on a rampage!

Brian Hansbury

Hey @alleyesonbree, how do I get you not to kill us when we come back to campus?

"Hey," Willow said as she dumped a pile of dirty laundry from her duffle bag in a pile on the floor.

"Hey."

It had been three days, and Tristan still hadn't come back. Hamlet's Ghost had been silent, and I was convinced it was because Tristan was waiting somewhere, ready to do something even worse. But there was nothing I could do to make people believe me. I'd even gone to Ms. Robinette to speak with her, but all she did was refer me to the guidance office. As if *they* could help me.

Willow browsed her closet, pulling out a few dresses and skirts and shoving them into her bag. She'd been staying with Vanessa since the vigil.

"See you later," she said.

"Yup." I didn't bother to look up.

Willow headed out the door, and I stood up and stretched. At our rehearsal last night, Mr. O'Dell had urged Eric and me to get together and rehearse. Eric had nodded in agreement, but had then brushed past me as he left the theater, Kennedy's hand clutched tightly in his. Onstage, we were all right, but I knew it wasn't coming together. And I knew there was no way it would, unless I could prove that I wasn't involved in the deaths.

Just then, the door swung back open.

"What'd you forget?" I asked Willow. Then I realized she wasn't alone.

Trailing behind her was my mother.

"Briana!" My mom swooped in and hugged me while Willow stood, silent and statue-like, by her side.

"I found her as I was heading out," Willow explained.

"What are you doing here?" I asked in disbelief.

"Well, I *tried* calling you, but your phone was off."

"We had no *power*."

"Fresh Maine air makes everything better, don't you think, girls?" my mother said as she swept past me and opened the window. She glanced disapprovingly at my side of the room. While Willow's own wall was decorated with artsy Instagram photos she'd printed out herself, mine was empty except for the single poster advertising the MacHale one-act festival from the fall.

"What are you doing here?" I asked again.

"Well, the parent organization sent an e-mail alert about Skye's tragic accident and the electricity investigation. So of course I was worried . . . and then I ended up doing some research on the website to see how I could get in touch with you if your phone was out of power . . . and found that article about the play auditions and how horrible they must have been for you. Darling, why didn't you *tell* me what a hard time you're having?" Mom's eyes were wide.

"Because I'm fine. Because it's . . ." I exhaled. "I'm fine."

"I'll go," Willow announced. "Nice to meet you, Mrs. —"

"Oh, don't leave! I just wanted to come and give Briana some TLC, but of course, that extends to her best friends as well. Would you like to come to lunch with us?"

"I couldn't." Willow shook her head, her expression making it obvious how creeped out she was by the term *best friends*.

"Well, let me at least take a picture of you girls. Briana, please look a little more cheerful!" Mom commanded as if I were a five-year-old. Automatically, I obliged, stepping closer to Willow as Mom took a picture with her iPhone.

"Thanks! I'm sure Briana told you how I was a Macolyte myself, back in the day."

"I didn't know that. But Bree keeps a lot of secrets," Willow said icily.

I held my breath. She wouldn't say anything about the Twitter account. Would she?

"What do you mean? She's not having trouble fitting in, is she?" Mom frowned.

"Everything's fine," I said quickly. "I just woke up. And I'm supposed to rehearse today, so maybe you should go."

"Rehearse?" Mom's eyes flickered. "What do you mean?"

"Um, I'm playing the Ophelia understudy now."

"You are?" Mom boomed. "Why didn't you tell me? Oh, Bree, that's wonderful!"

Willow's expression darkened.

"It's not that . . . wonderful, actually. At all."

But Mom didn't seem to notice my discomfort. "Well, this calls for a celebration! Willow, you'll come with us to lunch?" Mom expectantly arched her perfectly groomed eyebrow up at me.

"No." Not bothering to be polite, Willow practically ran out of the room.

But Mom seemed oblivious to the drama swirling around her. "All right, then. Ready?" Mom asked brightly as we left the dorm. I kept quiet until we stepped off campus.

"What are you doing here?" I exploded. "It's been a really weird week, and this is not helping."

"Why don't you let me *try* to help?" She turned to me, her cheeks red from the cold. "Why didn't you tell me you were having problems here?"

"You don't even *know* the problems I'm having here!" I've seen people *die*. People talked about me behind my back. Someone was about to be murdered by my former friend and no one would believe me. And now my mother came to give it a kiss and make it all better?

Mom's face softened. "Tell me what's happening, honey. I'm here to listen."

"Let's just go to lunch," I said wearily.

Mom picked up her pace, clearly in her element as she walked along the salt-covered sidewalks toward town.

"We're going to the Sunrise Café," she announced, naming the trendy bistro facing the mill. It had a wraparound deck and overpriced pasta and was as out of place in Forsyth, Maine, as MacHale. It was popular with students, making it the last place on earth I wanted to go right now. I couldn't deal with more whispers and stares.

"No." I shook my head.

"What?" Mom narrowed her eyes at me.

"Please," I said. "Let's go somewhere else."

Mom mashed her lips together as though she were going to say something. But she didn't.

This time, I was the one who led the way, along the path of the river, in the opposite direction of town. Here, the sidewalks hadn't been salted. We walked up the hill to the Trusty Ax. I turned to see her reaction as the sign came into view, anticipating her lip curling in distaste before it happened.

"So this is where you all hang out now? How . . . authentic," Mom said, almost spitting out the word as she walked through the entranceway.

Inside, the bar was swarmed with middle-aged men watching the tiny corner TV. The air smelled like smoke, proving the sticker on the door with an illustration of a crossed-out cigarette was more a halfhearted suggestion than anything substantial.

"Quaint."

It was that word that made me march toward the corner booth that Eric and I had sat in the last time we were here. I knew that Eric was at rehearsal. But it still made me feel close to him. It made me feel like I had gone back in time, when all I had to worry about were auditions.

"Hey."

I glanced up as two laminate-covered menus thwacked down on the table. Standing at the table was Zach.

He gave me a crooked half smile.

"Hey, Bree. Good to see you. Sorry we didn't get more of a chance to talk the other night."

I nodded wordlessly, aware Mom was curiously watching both of us.

"So, things sound pretty intense over at MacHale. How are you doing? I'm Zach, by the way," he said as he turned to my mom.

"Do you have any specials?" Mom asked loudly.

"Oh. Yeah. They're up there." Zach jerked his chin up toward the handwritten list on a chalkboard above the bar. He stood there for another moment, then, when he realized neither my mom nor I were going to talk, he wandered away.

"You have a friend," Mom said, in the same tone of voice someone else might use to say *You have a rash.* "Who is he?"

"Zach," I said. "He just said his name two minutes ago."

"Does *Zach* have a last name?" My mother's voice was dripping with sarcasm.

"No, Mom. Only people in boarding school have last names. That's why they use them *all the time*."

"Well then." Mom sat and stared at me in stony silence. Even though the bar was raucous, no one was sitting in the restaurant area, making everything even more awkward between us. "You aren't yourself."

Before I could respond, Zach wandered back.

"What would you all like?"

"I'm not very hungry, I'm afraid," Mom said. "Just a tea."

"All right. What about you?" Zach's eyes lingered on me. I turned and looked out the window, toward the river.

"A grilled cheese, I guess?"

"She'll have a grilled cheese," Mom said. "And that's all," she added when Zach didn't immediately leave.

The silence settled between us again.

"Maybe the reason why you don't feel like you're fitting in as well as you could be is because you're focusing too much on your friendships with people who live in town. To the detriment of MacHale friendships."

"Mom!" I realized that the television in the front of the bar had been turned off and saw more than a few curious stares our way. I took a deep breath. "You have no idea what's going on."

"Well then, tell me."

I shook my head.

Just then, there was a commotion by the bar. Two guys in cop uniforms immediately sprang up from their lunch, running down the hill toward the river. Patrons crowded to the picture windows against the wall.

"What's happening?" Mom called out.

A grizzly looking lumberjack-like guy turned to face us.

"Looks like they found a body."

I elbowed my way to the front of the crowd and pressed my face against the plate glass. I saw two officers carefully holding what looked like a limp, long limbed boy.

And I saw a bright blue streak in the water-drenched hair.

My knees buckled and I nearly collapsed, holding my knees with my hands for support.

Tristan was dead.

CHAPTER 14

Zach Mathis

Hey @alleyesonbree, can we talk? Meet me at the Nautilus at eight?

Called "the Nauseous" by MacHale students, the Nautilus was a run-down diner on the far end of Main Street. I'd never had any reason to go. And I was amazed I was able to get off campus tonight, especially when the school was on lock-down. Luckily, I'd managed to convince Ms. Robinette I was with my mother, while convincing my mom that she needed to leave so I could "process" Tristan's death with my friends. I was free to go wherever I wanted. And here I was, meeting Zach Mathis. I needed to know why he'd been looking for Tristan the night of the party.

As soon as I entered I spotted Zach slouched in a corner booth, his baseball cap low over his eyes.

I slid in across from him.

"So?" I asked, my voice on edge.

"Was that guy a friend of yours? Tristan?"

"Was he a friend of *yours*?" I countered. Tristan's words floated into my head. *Hamlet's Ghost is hiding in plain sight.* Or on the other side of town. Why hadn't Tristan told me Zach was Hamlet's Ghost?

Zach nodded. He flexed his fingers to crack his knuckles, and I caught sight of a few still-healing cuts on his hands. Zach noticed my gaze and balled them into fists, so the angry, raised red marks were out of my sight.

But they weren't out of my mind. I couldn't help but wonder how he'd gotten the cuts, and whether they were the result of rewiring the MacHale auditorium to electrocute Skye or getting into a struggle with Tristan as he tried to push him in the river.

"I spoke with Tristan a couple of times. He said he was working on a story."

"Yup." My eyes darted back and forth. I expected that someone would jump out of the shadows at any moment, or a group of MacHale kids would burst in, ready to yank me out from the diner and push *me* into the river. Or Zach would reach across the table and strangle me. Anything was possible. I took a deep breath.

"Do either of you want something to eat?" An ancient gray-haired waitress shuffled up to our table.

Both of us shook our heads.

She narrowed her eyes. "Can't sit if you don't eat."

"Fine. A coffee," Zach said.

"Me too."

"Anyway, Tristan said he was working on a story about the Sarah Charonne murder, and how that made the relationship between MacHale and Forsyth complicated. He spoke with Kevin McGinty. . . . You know, that auto mechanic who everyone said murdered Sarah."

"Mmhmm . . ." I trailed off as the waitress plunked our two mugs of coffee on the table.

"Anyway, Kevin said that he didn't do it."

"I'm sorry, but do you think I care about a decades-old murder?" I exploded. "I came because I thought you'd have information about MacHale now. People are dying!"

Heads swiveled to look at me, and I lowered my voice.

"I know people are dying." Zach lowered his voice. "That's why I care. That's why I'm talking to you. It's not just about your little boarding school anymore."

"So what else did he tell you?"

"That there was another guy. One they never questioned. He was another Forsyth kid. His name was Matthew Lampert. But he disappeared after graduation. People thought he'd killed himself, but Kevin told Tristan that he didn't believe it. So Tristan did some digging, and found that Matthew may still be alive. Except that he's using a different name these days." Zach's mouth twisted into a wry smile. "Any guesses?"

I shook my head as I took a sip of flavorless coffee. I was done playing games.

"Breckin O'Dell."

"What?" I sputtered, as coffee shot out of my mouth. "What are you talking about?"

"Breckin O'Dell is completely made up. His real name is Matthew Lampert. It makes sense, right? Jilted crush from the wrong side of the tracks wants to get back at the girl he loved, so he kills her, then takes revenge on everything she stood for."

I refused to let anyone pull the wool over my eyes again. "Couldn't the same thing also apply to you? I mean, weren't you with Kennedy?"

Zach's expression darkened. "We were a theater couple. You know how that is. You rehearse with them, you date them.

Kennedy's good at those relationships." He laughed darkly to himself. "But this is bigger than Kennedy. And it's bigger than me getting kicked out from the auditions. This is Mr. O'Dell going nuts. And in plain sight, too. Seriously, I have some stuff from Tristan. I just needed to pull it together and then Tristan and I would —"

" 'Tristan and I'?" I interrupted. "No offense, but Tristan hated townies. I don't really think he'd volunteer to team up with one."

The corner of Zach's mouth tugged down.

"Be that as it may . . . when Tristan disappeared, I started doing my own research on this O'Dell guy," Zach said. "And I talked to the theater group he worked with in New York. They fired him from a production of *Macbeth* after someone died. Don't you think it's sort of a coincidence Skye got electrocuted in a play he's working on?" He raised an eyebrow.

"It just shows that it's easy to murder people backstage . . . if you're not afraid to get your hands dirty." My gaze fell toward Zach's balled fists. In response, he shoved his hands under the table and gave me a hard stare of his town.

"Look, Bree, I was pissed when I didn't get to audition. And I did date Kennedy back in the day. But I don't care enough about some school production to kill for it. But I get what you're thinking. That's what Tristan thought, too. That's why he reached out to me at first. But as soon as we talked, he realized I wasn't the murderer. So we started doing some research."

"On O'Dell," I said flatly.

"*No.* On Matthew Lampert. Who just so happened to disappear right after Sarah Charonne died."

"Okay, so what?"

"So, then Breckin O'Dell suddenly bursts onto the scene. When you look up his name, all of his plays come up . . . and some geneaology record about a guy who died in the 1800s. In *Forsyth*."

I nodded. "I've seen that gravestone," I said quietly. My mind swirled. Was Zach telling the truth, or was this an elaborate lie to get me off his trail? "So you think . . ."

"Matthew Lampert became Breckin O'Dell," Zach finished.

"So, what now? I asked.

"What do you mean, what now? We catch him. You know the passageways. We can go to his office and look on his computer and . . . something. That's what Tristan and I were going to do. He killed Tristan. I know it."

"What about the police?"

"The police?" Zach scoffed. "No. They won't believe us. *We* need to catch O'Dell."

"Why *we*?"

"Don't you see?" Zach leaned in. "We're not safe on our own. I know people are accusing you. And people at Forsyth are accusing me. The only way we can make sure we're safe is to have each other's backs."

"What about Tristan's back? You didn't have that, did you?"

Zach shook his head. "He shouldn't have gone alone. But he wanted . . ."

"Wanted to get murdered?"

"No!" Zach sighed in frustration. "He wanted the credit. He wanted it to be his story. And he paid the price."

I pushed myself away from the table. "I need to go."

"Of course you do. You don't believe me, do you?"

"I need to think, Zach. I need to think and I need to take care of myself."

"And you think I'm a murderer. Great. I knew I shouldn't trust you."

"Likewise," I said tightly. I pushed myself from the booth and stormed out of the diner.

CHAPTER 15

Briana Beland @alleyesonbree
The show must go on. Final countdown to #machalehamlet opening night.

Matt Jasinski
Who's going to be left in the show once @alleyesonbree kills everyone?

The auditorium was silent as I walked in. Supposedly, this was tech week — the week where lighting and sets were put in place. Tech rehearsals were tedious to sit through, which is why they were usually broken up by card games backstage, junk food runs, and silly pranks.

I winced, remembering how during the tech rehearsals for the one-act festival the big joke had been to string up a large pink stuffed plastic flamingo in a noose somewhere backstage. What had seemed silly was now incredibly macabre.

"All right, folks." Mr. O'Dell clapped his hands loudly, even though it wasn't necessary — everyone was already focused on the stage. I noticed Kennedy and Eric sitting together, his arm draped around her shoulders. My stomach clenched. I knew I shouldn't even be *thinking* about my crush on Eric at a time like this, but it seemed like my body hadn't gotten the message.

"I know this is a tough time. And I have no doubt that all of you will rise to the challenge. Remember the world Shakespeare wrote in. He wrote during the plague, during wars, during civil upset. He wrote knowing that his audience *and* his players had no idea if they, or if even their world as they knew it, would exist the next morning. They lived in a world where the stakes were high. And now, you live in that world, too. And instead of mourning it, use it as an opportunity for art."

I shifted, preparing for the inevitable glares that would come my way on the mention of the deaths by looking down at my lap. I wasn't sure if I agreed with that. Sure, knowing what true terror felt like made it easier to *act* terrified . . . but who would actually choose to live like this?

"And now let's get to work. I need Gertrude and Claudius, please!" Vivy Brownslee and Christian Kent clambered onstage.

Christian launched into his opening monologue, where Claudius gloats about his marriage to Gertrude, stumbling over his lines.

"You have to really make it seem like you're in love, Christian. That you've *conquered* her. You're the lion, and she's the lioness. She's strong, but you're stronger, and she knows it. So show it!" Mr. O'Dell said passionately as Vivy and Christian stared at each other.

"Wait, am I supposed to *act* like a lion?" Christian asked in confusion. Mr. O'Dell sucked in his breath. I was sure he was about to launch into one of his lectures when I heard a loud creaking noise coming from the roof.

Someone gasped.

Christian and Vivy nervously looked up.

Mr. O'Dell slammed his binder shut in frustration and hopped onstage.

"Seriously?" he asked rhetorically, huffing out his cheeks. "This is Maine. It snows. Snow piles up on tree branches, then falls on the roof. That's all it was."

"Sorry," Vivy said. Her lower lip trembled. Even from my perch all the way in the back of the theater, it was clear she was about to cry.

"Get back to work!" Mr. O'Dell barked.

Afternoon turned to evening as the play slowly took form onstage. And I had to admit it was *good.* The lights were moody and uneven, making the stage look like a cavernous castle lit by candlelight. Eric's voice sounded hollow and that, coupled with his unnaturally pale skin and the dark circles under his eyes, made him look like a man on the brink of madness. At several points, I sat on the edge of my seat, wondering what would happen next, even though I knew.

At least I knew in the play. I had no idea what would happen next in my life.

Finally, at ten o'clock, three hours after rehearsal was supposed to have finished, Mr. O'Dell nodded. We were still one act from the end, but ten p.m. marked curfew, and even Mr. O'Dell couldn't mess with that.

"That's a wrap for now. I'll see you all tomorrow at three o'clock sharp. Bree?"

"Yes?" I called from my perch in the back.

"Good, you're here. Haven't heard much from you online. Keep up the social media stuff, okay? Have you and Eric had a chance to rehearse? I want you in tech tomorrow."

"No." I shook my head.

"Why not?"

Because Eric thinks I murdered his ex. "Just . . . busy."

Mr. O'Dell rolled his eyes skyward, obviously annoyed. "All right. Then the two of you hang back. I expect you both to at least get *some* work done on your scenes tonight."

"It's curfew," Eric said sharply.

"I will speak to your house monitors and let them know the situation. We're in tech week. We can't have curfew interfering with that. They'll just have to understand. Everyone else, you may go."

Wordlessly, people began packing up and filing out. I noticed that Kennedy stayed glued to her spot next to Eric.

"Ms. Clifford?" Mr. O'Dell asked, as he packed his own battered leather briefcase.

"What?" she asked.

"Why are you still here? Don't you have curfew?"

"*I* don't. I go to Forsyth. I want to stay."

Mr. O'Dell shook his head. "No. Just Eric and Bree."

"But . . ." Kennedy protested.

Eric tightened his jaw. "It's fine. I'm fine."

Kennedy finally nodded. She swung her bag over her shoulder and marched up the aisle, giving me a death glare as she walked by.

"All right," Mr. O'Dell said, satisfied when she'd left. "Just lock up when you're done."

"You're not staying?" Eric asked, the tremor in his voice making it obvious he was terrified. He wasn't the only one.

"Nope. Trivia night at the Trusty Ax." Mr. O'Dell grinned, then glanced between the two of us. "Don't tell me you two are nervous, are you? It was bad luck. Could have happened anywhere. You'll both be *fine.* If anything, think of this as character building." Grinning at us, Mr. O'Dell left the theater.

"And then there were two," Eric murmured.

I clambered toward the stage. As soon as my feet hit the wood, I relaxed. No matter how tense I was, the stage never failed me: I always felt better standing on it.

"I guess we should get this done, right?" Eric asked, not looking me in the eyes.

"We don't have to rehearse if you don't want."

"No, let's just do it. I mean, that's what you want, right?" There was a hard edge to his voice. "I guess this is, like, your dream, isn't it? Being able to play Ophelia. You don't care who it might hurt." He paced back and forth onstage as if he was performing a monologue. Each word sliced to the core of my being. I wanted to match his level of passion and scream at him, asking him how he dare think I had anything to do with the murders. But it didn't matter how he *could* think that about me. He *did* think that about me.

"Let's just rehearse," I said quietly.

"Okay. Act three, scene one?" he asked gruffly.

"Sure."

"Just wait backstage. I'll go through my monologue, then you enter from stage left."

I wordlessly headed toward the wings as Eric stood in the middle of the stage, performing the "To be, or not to be" monologue. I sat offstage and hugged my knees to my chest, allowing myself to get swept up in his words. And then, out of the corner of my eye, I saw a shadow shift in the wings across from where I sat.

I squinted. It wasn't a trick of the light. The shadow was crouching in the corner. Meanwhile, Eric was oblivious, his voice getting louder and more sure as he got caught up in the words of the monologue.

I tore my eyes away from Eric. Someone was there, in the wings. Someone was watching. I needed to do something. I would *not* have Eric die. Not here. Not now.

My gaze landed on the prop table, where swords of varying lengths were laid out for a sword fight.

I stealthily moved toward the table, then grabbed a sword. Of course it wasn't real. I tested its weight. But it was heavy.

Eric's monologue was winding down. I had to move quickly. My back hugging the black velvet curtain, I quickly edged my way around the perimeter of backstage, hoping that I would get there before the shadow did anything.

"The fair Ophelia! Nymph, in thy orisons be all my sins remembered."

One step. Two steps. I was coming to the corner that would bring me only feet from the shadow.

"Nymph, in thy orisons be all my sins remembered!" Eric said again, enunciating each word. "Briana, that's you. Where are . . . ?"

I turned the corner. The shadow crouched, half-hidden in the curtains. It was either now or never.

I squeezed my eyes shut, held the sword above my head, and slammed it down as hard as I could against the head of the shadow.

"Bree!" Eric yelled.

The shadow groaned, falling onto the dimly lit stage. Blood poured into his reddish hair.

"It's not me! Mr. O'Dell . . . Trying . . . Look backstage," the figure burbled onstage.

It was Zach.

Of *course*.

Zach lay writhing on the ground as I raced onto the stage. Eric blinked in bewilderment.

"He was watching you. I saw him. And then I found the sword and then . . ." The sword fell to the ground with a clatter, and I realized that my arms and legs were shaking. Eric threw his arms around me, and I allowed my face to rest on his shoulder. When I pulled away, I realized that his shirt was damp with my tears.

I glanced down at Zach. He was curled into a ball, making guttural groaning noises.

"We need to call the police. *Now.* Before he gets up."

Eric broke out of his reverie and nodded. Then he looked back at me.

"I am so *sorry*, Bree. I just thought . . ."

"We need to *call the police*!" I roughly shoved Eric's shoulders.

"Right." Eric pulled out his cell and called 9-1-1 as I glanced down at Zach, still writhing in pain. Of course he'd been the killer. And he'd almost killed *Eric*. Why hadn't I called the police right after my meeting with him at the diner?

I knew why, of course. Because even now, after everything, I'd wanted a chance at playing Ophelia.

The wail of police sirens interrupted my thoughts. As the police and paramedics swarmed in, I sank back in Eric's arms, feeling more relieved and at home than I had in a long time.

CHAPTER 16

"Look, I'm *really* sorry about everything," Willow said.

"It's all right."

She'd been saying she was sorry since the moment that the police had come to take Zach away a week ago. But the police hadn't been able to prove anything. They'd confiscated his iPhone and laptop, but it would take weeks before they'd be able to dig through the data. And even though Hamlet's Ghost hadn't Tweeted recently, it didn't mean that he was gone.

Meanwhile, life at MacHale went on, with few of the students who *hadn't* been there over winter break aware of the terror that had struck the campus. Sure, they'd read about the murders, but the MacHale PR team had made the three deaths sound more like an unfortunate series of accidents than anything. And while one or two kids had decided to transfer to another school, the full dorms, class schedule, and extracurriculars every night of the week made it feel like the #machaledrama was over.

For most people, at least.

"So, are you excited for tomorrow?" Willow continued, oblivious to my mood. "You're going to be amazing!"

"We have to get through tonight first."

"Right, but that'll be awesome, too! I'm *really* glad that you're in the play. The sheer dress looks great on you. I mean, I *knew* it would." Willow narrowed her eyes at me. "Are you *sure* you're okay?"

"Yes," I responded testily. Just last week, Willow had been so sure that I was a serial killer that she'd moved out of our room, without ever even *trying* to listen to my side. And now, everything was fine? It wasn't that simple. After all, I was the same person I'd been the whole time. Only now, I'd just been launched into the popularity stratosphere. And while it was a million times better than notoriety, at the end of the day, it was still people making snap judgments about things I had very little control over.

Yes, I'd discovered Zach sneaking around backstage, likely getting ready to cause another "accident." Yes, I'd saved Eric. But I hadn't saved Andi, or Skye, or Tristan. Their deaths were never officially ruled as murders. And I couldn't shake the feeling that Hamlet's Ghost was *somewhere* out there, even now, when the entire campus looked postcard perfect, complete with snow dusting the paths and the winter sun glimmering off the pond.

Wordlessly, I walked through the stage door and into the backstage bustle.

I held my phone in my hand, prepared to take any pictures, Tweet any last-minute backstage observations, or respond to any questions that the ticket-buying public out front may have.

"Hey, can you take a picture of the two of us?" Kennedy tugged my elbow toward a corner where Eric was standing. He wore a black suit and loafers with a red tie, suitable for Mr. O'Dell's vision of Hamlet as a young and privileged son of a corporate CEO. Kennedy wore a knee-length ivory white slip. One of its straps kept falling down her shoulder. She was barefoot. Mr. O'Dell wanted Ophelia to look like a selfie-obsessed girl lounging around her parents' home during a break from college.

Despite the sadness surrounding the production, I felt a glimmer of excitement that tomorrow, *I* would be the one in the costume next to Eric.

"You look great," I said to Kennedy, a lump in my throat. Eric had been nothing but friendly to me since the night of our rehearsal, and he'd even sent a dozen roses to my dorm the morning after. But that was all he was: friendly. It seemed like realizing Zach had been the murderer had made him let go of his guilt over Skye. Or maybe it was because Kennedy was Zach's ex, and she was legitimately freaked out over his entire unsavory past and needed a shoulder to cry on. Whatever the reason, the two of them had been virtually inseparable. There was no way I could come between them. Onstage, Eric would cup Kennedy's chin in his hand in a way that was so tender that I felt my heart melt a bit. They belonged together.

Eric and Kennedy smiled, and I took the photo.

"All right, let's circle up!" Mr. O'Dell shouted. He was clad all in black leather pants and a tight black t-shirt. A fedora was cocked at a jaunty angle on his head. One by one, everyone shuffled into a circle around him.

"Good. Now, I know we've had a hard few weeks. But we've emerged stronger than ever. So let's show everyone what a force MacHale and Forsyth can be and give the audience a performance they'll never forget!" he said to enthusiastic cheers.

I Tweeted a picture of him giving his *Let's do this!* speech, then took my place in the wings to watch the show.

Seconds after Kennedy made her first appearance, she staggered toward me, her face white.

"Are you all right?" I asked, terror already clutching my heart.

"I don't feel that great," she whispered. She took a few more steps before leaning against the concrete wall. Eric was standing center stage, and I could just make out the audience leaning toward him in rapt attention.

"Maybe it's nerves?"

"Maybe. It's just my stomach *kills*." Kennedy patted her abdomen. "Like, I feel like I'm being sliced with knives from the inside."

"Maybe get some water?" I whispered, shrugging helplessly. I was backstage to Tweet amusing anecdotes in real time, not to get distracted by a stage fright crisis.

"Right. Good idea."

I turned my attention back to the show. Three scenes later, I felt a hand on my shoulder. It was Sabrina Stokes, one of the stage crew members.

"You're on!" She whispered.

"What?"

"Kennedy feels really sick. She doesn't think she can go on. We're trying to find Mr. O'Dell to let him know, but in the meantime, you need to get into costume. Now. You don't have much time."

"I'm on?" I repeated.

"Yeah. *Soon.* I think you've got about two scenes, but they go by fast. Hurry up."

I raced from the wings and into the backstage area, shrugging off my cardigan along the way.

"Willow?" I called. "Anyone know where Willow is?" I asked a few of the cast members who were milling around. Kennedy lay on a big green couch at the far end of the space, groaning. Her hand rested on her forehead.

"I think she's up in the loft with the costumes," Leah offered.

Kennedy struggled to sit up. "Wait . . . I might be okay . . ." She said weakly, flopping back down. My heart twisted. I felt disloyal going onstage when she was sick, but the show had to go on. And I was her understudy. It wasn't like I'd poisoned her. It wasn't like she was poisoned at all. It was nerves, plain and simple. And I needed to stop worrying about Hamlet's Ghost and start thinking about my performance.

I hurried up the stairs, feeling a vague stirring of excitement beneath my guilt. I also wished my mom were there to see my star turn.

The perimeter of the already dim loft was filled with roll-away iron clothing racks that held the costumes. I knew my dress was somewhere, but I needed Willow to help me sort through the racks and find it.

"Willow?" I called again, deeper in the racks, which extended from the costume cage. I took a few steps forward before my foot got caught on a piece of crushed black velvet. I stumbled, catching myself with my hands as my knees landed on something hard.

I tugged at the fabric, looked down, and gasped.

It was a piece of plywood, painted gray. The words KENNEDY CLIFFORD were written in red ink, deliberately drippy to look like blood.

And then, all of a sudden, everything clicked into place. The BRECKIN O'DELL gravestone. Zach's nonsensical ramblings. Mr. O'Dell's insistence we act as though we had life-and-death stakes in the performance. Because we did. He was killing his performers. He was staging the ultimate tragedy.

He was Hamlet's Ghost.

"Kennedy?" I heard Mr. O'Dell's voice from below my perch in the loft.

I squeezed myself in between the rows of costumes, getting lost in lace and tulle. My heart thumped against my chest so loudly I was sure Mr. O'Dell could hear it. He had poisoned Kennedy. It was so clear. And if I went onstage, he'd poison me, too. Unless I did something. Fast. But all I could do was stand rooted to my spot, watching him.

"What's wrong with her?" he asked, as his gaze fell on her prone form on the couch.

"She doesn't feel good," Leah Banks said importantly. "I've been *telling* her to drink water, but she won't."

Mr. O'Dell's eyes narrowed as Kennedy writhed on the couch.

"What did you do?" he demanded.

"Nothing! Well, I drank a sip of the prop juice because I wanted to make sure it tasted gluten-free. They got the wrong kind last time. And if I have to drink a whole glass later . . . well, I wanted to make sure it was right."

"You drank the prop wine?" Mr. O'Dell asked.

Kennedy nodded before turning over and heaving onto the concrete floor. The small group of kids surrounding her groaned and jumped away, but Mr. O'Dell stood rooted in his spot, his arms crossed and his expression darkening.

"All right, Plan B. Make sure Briana Beland is in costume and *ready*. I have my cue now. Briana's a lucky girl, I suppose."

I balled my fists together, trying to drum up my courage. I needed to save myself. I needed to save the rest of the cast. And I still couldn't tear my eyes away from the drama unfolding before my eyes.

"She's getting ready, I think," Leah squeaked.

I pressed myself farther into the costumes. It was all so ridiculously clear now. Mr. O'Dell had been Hamlet's Ghost from day one. He had been Tweeting in plain sight and none of us had noticed, because we were too wrapped up in our own dramas. And now he'd planned to poison Kennedy and the rest of the cast, one by one, as each of them drank from the prop wine.

The ground shook as Mr. O'Dell clambered up the steps and toward the metal catwalk that connected the loft to the rickety iron pathway that connected the backstage area to the front of the theater.

"Stupid fools . . . the last time I work with students . . ." he muttered to himself as he arranged his headset. A few feet away from me, he stopped, glancing at the pile of plywood headstones, which were still askew from when I tripped. He quieted as I held my breath.

Finally, he started walking again.

"Briana?" Leah's voice wafted upward. "I found Willow. Are you still up there?"

Mr. O'Dell paused again and glanced wildly around. I pressed my back farther against the dense crunch of materials. All of a sudden, I heard a loud clank.

The metal clothing rack I'd been pressing up against had bumped into another.

"Bree?"

Mr. O'Dell's voice was soft and smooth, my name sounding almost like a prayer from his lips.

I crossed my fingers and mashed my lips together. I couldn't hear the onstage monitor because of the amount of noise backstage. I hoped that meant Mr. O'Dell couldn't hear me.

"Mr. O'Dell?" a voice called up the stairs. "Your cue."

He muttered something under his breath, then crept along the catwalk to the spot in the far left of the auditorium where his voice was supposed to boom out over the audience, making them think the ghost surrounded them.

This was my cue. I had to do something.

I couldn't call the police; that would take too long. I needed to do something *now*, while he was playing his part and couldn't hurt anyone.

I pushed myself out of the pile of costumes and followed behind him, my entire body trembling as I stepped on the rickety metal catwalk. Students weren't allowed to access it until they'd sat through a mandatory meeting by the MacHale safety officer *and* were always supposed to wear a harness. I never had done either, and I wasn't sure if the swaying I felt was because of the unsturdy walkway beneath my feet or my own terror.

Mr. O'Dell crouched in the corner, adjusted his microphone, and gazed intently at the stage. Onstage, across the audience from us, Eric looked up to our corner, his mouth opening in a wide O of shock when he realized that I was standing behind Mr. O'Dell. Noticing Eric's shock, Mr. O'Dell turned around.

"Whither wilt thou lead me? Speak. I'll go no further," Eric said, his gaze unwavering from my face.

Mr. O'Dell turned from me to Eric, and back to me.

There was a pause.

"Your cue, Mr. O'Dell," I heard a thin, tinny, disembodied voice leaking through Mr. O'Dell's headset. He took a deep breath and turned back toward the stage.

And then I closed my eyes and pushed Mr. O'Dell's shoulders. The headset made an ear-piercing shriek, but Mr. O'Dell didn't make a sound as he tumbled twenty feet from the catwalk onto the aisle below, where he landed with a thud.

For one second, there was silence, the same type of collective silence that occurs at the end of a play, when the spell is broken and the audience returns to their real lives. Normally, this moment is marked with a burst of applause, an acknowledgement of the fact that everything that happened in the past few hours was just pretend.

Only now, the half second of silence marked the realization that the audience was part of a terrible tragedy, one that would never, ever have a curtain.

And that's when the screams began.

EPILOGUE

Briana Beland @alleyesonbree

"The course of true love never did run smooth."

— A Midsummer Night's Dream

The sun dappled through the open sunroof of the theater, warming the stage. I stepped onto a masking tape X in the center of the space and rolled my shoulders backward and forward, warming myself up for the opening-night curtain. Even though it was hours away, I liked being alone in the auditorium. Slowly, it had turned back into a safe space, away from the horror and sadness that had happened in the past few months.

It was also nice to stand onstage, especially since I'd spend the next few hours sitting in the front row, watching the show come together under my direction. *A Midsummer Night's Dream* was all about mistaken identities and magic, where everything comes together in the end and everyone is better off and happier than they were at the beginning of the play. It was the exact opposite of *Hamlet*, and all of us — those who'd survived and had stayed — hoped that this production could truly be the healing one to unite MacHale and Forsyth; that it would create a tribute to actors and actresses who'd had their lives cut short far too soon.

Breckin O'Dell — or rather, Matthew Lampert — was currently in a mental hospital. The police had quickly found the Hamlet's Ghost account on his computer. Tristan had been right: Hamlet's Ghost had been hiding in plain sight. And no one had realized it until it was far too late. Breckin . . . Matthew . . . whoever he was . . . had quickly confessed his crimes, proud of the body count, proud that he'd orchestrated a tragedy of his own creation that had, in his words, mattered.

Meanwhile, the Forsyth and MacHale students tentatively started to move forward. Zach Mathis had led the first meeting between the two schools, where we all agreed that the show must go on. But not *Hamlet*. We didn't need tragedy.

So we picked *A Midsummer Night's Dream*, and I found myself surprised to volunteer to direct the show. I liked the rhythm of helping actors find themselves in the parts, to see how their real-life experiences informed the way they connected to their characters onstage. I'd cast Eric and Kennedy as Oberon and Titania, the king and queen of the fairies. It made sense; in the past few months, they'd certainly become the king and queen of the MacHale-Forsyth theater world.

And they deserved that title. Kennedy had only drunk a small amount of the poisoned prop wine and had recovered, Eric by her side. Rather than being annoying, their couple status seemed to signify new hope for Forsyth and MacHale as everyone tried to wrap their minds around what had happened.

Besides, I didn't need Eric anymore.

"Hey." I felt a pair of hands circle my back. I relaxed into them, remembering a time when this gesture would have meant something much more ominous. Zach planted a kiss on the top of my head.

I turned to face him. Seeing him still made my stomach flutter, only this time, the feeling was good.

"You nervous?"

"You're not supposed to say *nervous*. You're supposed to say *excited*," I murmured as my lips brushed his. He kissed me back. We were standing in a shaft of sunlight, not the spotlight. There was no audience; no followers. And I wasn't sure how our story would end — whether it would be a five-act up-and-down drama or the equivalent of a lighthearted one-act. I didn't have the script. I wasn't even sure what part I was playing. All I knew was that I loved the role.

Anna Davies is a former magazine editor turned full-time writer. She's written for the *New York Times*, *New York*, *Elle*, *Glamour*, *Fitness*, *Self*, and other publications. Her novels include *Wrecked* and *Identity Theft*. She can usually be found in New York . . . and can always be found on Twitter.